Spence desperately wants Lori to face the truth of her past.

"Lorelei Sommers, you've been trying your whole life to live up to something you thought your daddy might eventually love. There is no love in people like him."

"So," she finally shot back, "I suppose now you want me to accept the love of your God? This wonderful Father? Let Him be the father to me that I never had, right?"

"Well, yes." Spence was slightly taken aback by her direct line of questioning. It seemed she had heard something of God before. . .although he was not sure he wanted to know just how or what she had learned.

"No thanks! I've had my fill of 'fathers' for this lifetime. That's why I'm leaving altogether. . ."

GLORIA BRANDT makes her home in Wisconsin with her husband and three young daughters. *Behind the Scenes* is her first inspirational romance novel. Gloria says "I always want to touch on the salvation message in my books. . .and in the process, encourage people that no matter what their circumstances or background, there is hope."

Behind the Scenes

Gloria Brandt

Heartsong Presents

To Sara,
for modeling the way to go.

And a very special thank you to Sally.
Mere words will never express my gratitude
for your patience, encouragement, and devotion.

A note from the Author:
I love to hear from my readers! You may write to me at the following address:

Gloria Brandt
Author Relations
P.O. Box 719
Uhrichsville, OH 44683

ISBN 1-55748-868-1

BEHIND THE SCENES

Cover illustration by Kay Salem.

PRINTED IN THE U.S.A.

one

"Spring, indeed!" Lori muttered as the heavy, metal door slammed shut against the whirling snow. "Whoever heard of snow at the end of April?"

She brushed the cold, white flakes from her leather jacket. Stamping her freezing feet to try and regain some feeling in them, she seriously began to wonder why she had opted to come to Minneapolis when Florida had been so much warmer. She glanced around the auditorium of the Penny Lane Theater, noticing the crystal chandeliers were dimly lit, awaiting the upcoming performance.

A babble of voices drifted up from the orchestra pit where several of the cast and crew were barely visible from the lowered area.

It was then she heard the music. As she made her way down the slightly sloping aisle, she picked out several jazzy, ragtime tunes. Whoever was playing was good. She reached the partition that separated the pit from the front row of the auditorium and rested her arms on the low railing while she continued to listen to the banter taking place around the baby grand. The throng around the mystery player was too thick for her to see through, so she sighed and settled back into one of red velvet seats to enjoy the lively melodies.

Closing her eyes, she let the sprightly notes engulf her. Lori had always been amazed at the redemptive powers of music. Her eyes slowly fluttered open and she studied the expansive, molded ceiling, trimmed in the gold so reminiscent of the twenties when Penny Lane had been built.

She had to smile when the opening notes of "The Entertainer" graced the empty auditorium. What a grand showplace this theater must have been back then! She could almost envision the people decked out in their finest attire to attend one play or symphony or another.

With the last note, the present came crashing back, unbidden. Her cohorts broke into enthusiastic applause and laughter, then finally broke away and headed for different areas of the theater.

Lori jumped up and followed those who were on their way to makeup, but not before she got a good look at the Scott Joplin wanna-be at the keys. He did not look familiar, but she took a moment to study him anyway. He was just an average looking guy. Brown hair, medium height, medium build. . .average. But he did have on a pair of black Wayfarer sunglasses at which Lori rolled her eyes.

Oh, too cool, she smirked. Shaking her head, she walked a bit faster. Tonight was the theater's last performance of *Our Town,* and she had better hurry.

"It's about time, Miss Sommers." The low voice came from the dark recesses of backstage.

"Hi, Gary," she replied flatly as she continued to dig through the rack for her costume.

"How do you always know it's me?" His towering body moved into the soft light cast from the side door.

"Well, who else would be back here trying to bother me in the dark?"

"Almost everyone I know," he replied with a slight chuckle in his tone.

Lori involuntarily stiffened. She paused for a moment before reminding herself he only told the truth. "Yeah, whatever." She yanked her skirt and blouse from the hanger and began to head toward the backstage steps.

"Hey, wait." Gary grabbed her arm, forcing her to turn toward him again. "Are we on for tonight?"

"What do you mean?" She sighed with impatience, although

she fully knew his meaning.

He made no effort to keep his faded blue eyes from roving up and down her figure. “You know,” he said, leaning an arm across the line of clothes, “we could celebrate our final performance. Have our *own* little cast party.” His insinuating grin accentuated the deep cleft in his chin.

Although Gary was acting no different from his usual, overly familiar self, Lori felt perturbed. “No thanks, Gary. I’m really pretty beat from these shows. I don’t even think I’ll take in the planned cast party tonight. I just want to go home and relax for a while.”

“You sure?” His eyebrows rose along with the tone of his voice in obvious disappointment.

“Yeah. . .yeah,” she reiterated, more sure than ever it was just what she needed. She had not spent any time alone in a long time.

“Okay,” Gary reluctantly agreed. “But. . . ,” he touched his index finger to her nose, “I’ll expect to hear from you soon.”

She turned away, half in disgust, but his quick hands spun her around once again. Any protests she might have hoped to voice were smothered in his heavy, possessive kiss. Managing a grim smile before exiting, she nearly ran to the long-awaited escape down the short flight of steps. She raked her arm across her mouth, trying to remove the pressure that still seemed to remain.

Funny, how only a month ago I welcomed that. Lori shook her head in wonderment as she entered the brightly illuminated room that smelled of cake makeup and hair spray.

“Hi, Lori.”

“Hey, Erica.” Lori patted the petite girl on the shoulder, trying to avoid the deadly mist of hair spray that hovered around her friend’s head.

“All set for tonight?” Erica Stevens shook out her black curls and rechecked her lipstick in the lighted mirror.

“Yeah, I guess so. It’ll be nice to be done, finally.”

"Going to the cast party?" Erica's already large, brown eyes widened as she expertly brushed mascara upward on her long lashes.

"I don't think so." Lori began to discard her sweat shirt and jeans.

"Really?" Erica finally took the opportunity to look at Lori. "They've decided to have it at the Regency."

"Yeah, I know. It's supposed to be a pretty ritzy place, I guess."

"I guess?" Erica added sarcastically. "I should have the bucks to frequent such a place all the time." Her eyes took on a curious glow as she studied Lori. "Why don't *you* go there more often?"

Lori shrugged, finished buttoning up her blouse, and threw her wad of clothes into a pile under the makeup table. "Got sick of places like that a long time ago, I suppose."

"Ah. . .the price you pay when you're the daughter of a man in political circles."

Lori shot her friend a quick look. "Yeah, and you can keep that quiet, remember?"

"Sure, sure. I still don't know what the big deal is, though," Erica said as she waved Lori off nonchalantly. "I'm quiet."

Lori managed a small look of relief that she did not quite feel. "Better scoot. I see Maggie's waiting for me." She nodded toward the gray-haired woman in the far corner of the room.

"Hey," Erica interrupted Lori's short walk. "If you change your mind. . .Regency. Gary might be disappointed if you don't show."

Lori tucked a strand of forever-wayward hair behind her ear and sighed. "Let Gary worry about his own life for once." She saw her friend's eyes flare in surprise, but she merely continued picking up her things from the table in silence.

Lori whirled around and stalked over to her waiting chair. Now, why did she go and snap? Her current mood was not Erica's fault. Maybe if everybody would just lay off about Gary. They seemed to think that he and she were some sort of item. The thought gave Lori a panicked, smothered feeling. They had been seeing each other for a month or so. Maybe it was time for a break. With a sigh, she flopped down in front of the lighted mirror.

"Good evening, Lori."

She managed a smile for the plump, cheerful woman staring down at her. "Hi, Maggie."

"Last show, dear." She began to set Lori's waist-length blond hair in hot rollers as she chattered merrily at her. "Did I hear you say you're not going to the party tonight?"

Lori started to nod her head but stopped when she felt her hair pull. "That's right. Are you?"

"I don't think so." Maggie frowned as she shook her head. "I don't feel real comfortable in places like that. I'm more of a homebody."

Lori had no comment for that. She definitely could not identify with being a homebody. Fact was, she did not really seem to fit in anywhere.

As Maggie started on the makeup, Lori closed her eyes and remained silent. She was never quite sure of what to say around Maggie. The older woman was different from a lot of the others at the theater. Sure of herself. . .something that made Lori very ill at ease.

She sighed and tried to break the awkward silence. "Um, who was the guy on the piano out there?"

Maggie's round face lit up. "Oh, that was Spence. Isn't he wonderful?"

"Yeah, he plays pretty well. But who is he?"

Maggie stepped back with the large powder brush in hand. "Why, Lori. That's Spencer Berg."

"Oh." Lori felt her face warm. Well, how was she to know who he was? She had never seen him before, the famous Spencer Berg. Lori had been with Penny Lane for only the last year, but from what she had heard of him, he could do no wrong. He had starred in most of the plays, but his expertise seemed to be in the musicals. Apparently his voice-and song-writing skills were outstanding.

She remembered asking about him once and where he was, everyone had seemed pretty quiet, almost sad about it, just stating he had had some sort of accident. She recalled his lively playing in the pit only a while earlier. Whatever had happened to him, he certainly seemed okay now.

Maggie put on the last touch of lipstick. "Okeydoke, Lori. You're set."

"Thanks, Maggie." Lori stood and grabbed a nearby copy of the script. She really did not need to study her lines, she knew them well enough by now. But maybe it would keep her mind busy on other things besides Gary, and Erica's comments, and. . .everything.

❧

Spence clasped his hands together and pushed them outward to stretch his fingers. It felt good to be at this piano again. It had been far too long. He smiled to himself, remembering everyone's reaction. They had sounded pleased to have him back. He had certainly missed this little family. Sliding his sleeve up slightly, he pressed the small button on his watch. "The time is 6:02 P.M." There was still an hour until show time. Maybe he would go and bug Mike for a while.

Locating the roughly textured banister, he easily moved up the familiar narrow stairs to what at one time had been a private viewing stand for dignitaries who attended the various plays and operas. Now, with nineties technology and also what Spence considered unsentimental necessity, the grand balcony had been enclosed and shaped into a sound and light booth. With a melancholy sigh, he shoved open the heavy door.

"Howdy, Spence," his friend's cheery voice welcomed him. "Gettin' bored already?"

"Nah, just antsy. Anything I can do up here?"

"Sure. You wanna work the lights?"

Spence could almost hear the smile in Mike's teasing voice.

"Okay. If you don't mind having the spots on the ceiling or somewhere in the audience," Spence tossed back, good-naturedly. "Well-l-l. . . ," Mike drawled, as though he were seriously considering the proposition, "maybe you can help man the headset instead. You in the mood for bossing the back-stage people around?"

"Hand it over." Spence held out his open hand and fit the device snugly on his head, positioning the tiny microphone toward his mouth. "Thanks. I'll have to say, though, the babygrand down there felt much more comfortable."

Mike was quiet for several moments. "You still sound really good, Spence. Next show it's your turn, right?"

"Yep. Can't wait."

"Good to have you back, man."

Spence just smiled.

❧

Lori shuffled into the wings and plunked down onto the nearest chair. She could feel the perspiration trickling down her back, and she moved back and forth against the chair to try and alleviate some of the dampness.

"Nice job, Lori," several minor characters whispered as they skittered past her. She smiled. She was tired, but it was a good kind of tired. The kind one feels after accomplishing something worthwhile. She realized the only time she really felt good was when she was out under those lights, pretending to be somebody else, she mused. She heard the thunderous applause of the sold-out crowd, and it lifted her worn spirit.

"Okay, Lori, you're up," Tom, the stage manager, whispered as he beckoned with his hand.

Lori slowly rose and took a deep breath. Taking a quick wipe at her brow, she marched onto the wooden-plank stage and waited for the curtains to rise. This was old hat now. For the last several productions, she had been asked to sing a few numbers from the twenties and thirties to commemorate the anniversary of the opening of the Penny Lane Theater. She liked these songs; they were lilting and just fun. It now dawned on her how the earlier numbers she had heard Spencer Berg play had keyed her up for this even more than usual.

She heard the audience grow silent amid a few hushes and heard the now-familiar, soft hum of the motor that gracefully pulled up the expansive, crimson curtain. The orchestra began the intro, and she watched the director's slight baton carefully, though she knew exactly when to come in. She was part of this music.

❧

"Okay, blue lights. . .on!" Spence heard Mike deftly flipping switches as the orchestra opened into the first number. He quietly removed his headset and placed it on the board in front of him. He waited, listening for the soloist. When her strong and clear soprano broke through the sound room speakers he nearly gasped aloud. He wanted to ask who it was, but he was too mesmerized. All he could do was sit back and bask in the rich tones she seemed to throw out effortlessly.

After she had gone through "Blue Moon," "Embraceable You," and "Someone to Watch Over Me," Spence found himself on his feet, applauding with the rest of the enthusiastic audience. He was suddenly aware where he still was and promptly sat back down amid Mike's amused laughter, sending a grin in a half-hearted apology.

"Who *was* that?" he finally asked after he knew Mike had flipped on the house lights and the crowd had started to depart.

"Oh, her?" Mike sounded a little too blasé. "That's Lori."

"Oh, that's Lori," Spence mimicked. "Man, who is the girl with the angel voice?"

Mike laughed again, his easy chuckle. "Okay, okay. That was Lori Sommers. She's been here about a year. She's really got a set of pipes on her, huh?"

"This is what I've been missing?"

"Guess so."

"Wow." Spence was speechless for a few minutes. "Is she

going to be in the musical?" He hoped his tone did not sound too hopeful, but to have her as the lead. . . .

"I think so. She usually sticks around and does work on the backdrops, too."

"All that and an artist, too?" Spence shook his head in amazement.

"That's not half of it, buddy." Mike's voice contained a bit of suggestiveness.

"What do you mean?"

"Well, let me put it this way. Her full name is Lorelei Sommers. Are you familiar with German folklore?"

"Lorelei? Like the siren on the Rhine River that used to lure sailors' ships onto the rocks?" He heard Mike echo the last words with him. "What about it?"

"Um, she lives up to her namesake pretty well. She's even got the long, blond hair and green eyes to assist her in her 'catches'."

"She's a heartbreaker, huh?"

"Yep."

"So, has the mighty Mike Shelton had his heart broken by this temptress?" Spence teased.

"Nope. I stay away from mermaids like that."

Spence hated to make a judgment on someone he did not know. "Well, maybe a lot of it is hearsay. You know how rumors get flying around this place."

"Whatever. Let's go grab a burger or something. I'm starved." Mike eagerly jumped from his chair in his usual exuberant way.

Spence followed Mike back down the steps and into the now-silent auditorium.

"I'll be back in a second, Spence. I've gotta grab my coat in the dressing room."

"Okay, I'll wait here for you." Spence shuffled around on the thick carpeting lining the aisle and fiddled with his sunglasses until he heard someone enter the auditorium. He hastily replaced the dark shades. There were two people and they seemed to be arguing.

"Gary, just leave me alone! I said I don't want to go."

"But, why?" Spence recognized Gary Thomas's familiar, spoiled whine.

"Aren't the reasons I gave you before good enough? Or do I have to think up a batch of new ones?" The woman was obviously being pushed to her limit.

"Why don't you just tell me the real reason why you're not coming?"

"What are you talking about?"

"I've known about you since long before we started seeing each other. Why don't you just come out and say it?"

"Say what?" Her voice was a hushed scream.

"You've found a new toy to play with." Gary's voice was taunting, accusing.

There was the unmistakable smack of a hand cracking across flesh, then a very long silence.

"Hey, Spence, let's go." Mike had reentered the auditorium. He stopped at Spence's side before acknowledging the happy couple who seemed to have been oblivious to Spence's presence. "Hey, Gary, Lori. Wanna join us for some burgers?"

Spence tried to tug indiscreetly on his friend's arm, knowing Mike unaware of what had just taken place.

"No thanks," Gary answered rigidly.

"Lori?"

"Well, you know," she answered sweetly, "I might like that."

"I thought you were tired," Gary snapped.

"I am," Lori shot back. "But I have to eat sometime. Maybe I'll get my appetite back after you leave."

Mike cleared his throat and nudged Spence's arm. "We'll wait for you at the car, Lori."

"No need to wait," she said as she approached rapidly. "I'm finished here."

"Okay, let's go." Mike led the way as Spence felt Lori fall in step beside him.

two

Spence jerked backward, his hands to his ears, as the thunderous beat of a bass drum reverberated through his chest, clear down to his shoes.

"Nice place," he yelled over the screeching electric guitar. The acrid smell of cigarette smoke assaulted his nostrils, nearly making him choke on its thickness.

"Sorry," Mike answered in a similarly loud pitch. "I forgot tonight was band night at the Blue Heron. Is it that bad?"

"I'd rather not go deaf, too."

"Lori?" Mike directed his question to her.

"Yeah, I guess I could go for a more relaxing atmosphere tonight, too." Spence was more than relieved to hear her agree.

"Okay, I'll grab the burgers and we'll go to. . .Spence's!"

Mike was gone before Spence had a chance to respond. He sighed as he smiled at the spontaneity of his friend. He sat silent for a minute until he remembered he should be making conversation with the woman next to him.

"Lori?" he tried to say in a normal voice, but there was no response. "Lori?" He ventured again, reverting to the yell he had used before.

"Yeah?"

"Sorry." He shook his head and smiled. "Not the place to make small talk, I guess."

He heard her laugh in agreement, and they were silent again in the midst of the jungle of noise.

After they had sat for what seemed hours, Spence was beginning to wonder if Mike had left without them. He had certainly dumped them in the middle of an uncomfortable situation. Getting to know Lori a little better was certainly not encouraged in this atmosphere. Maybe there would be more of a chance at home. *Home.* He hoped that Corinne had been there and straightened up a bit.

"Well, short of nearly getting myself trampled over there, here's the food," Mike shouted above the growing din. "Let's go before there's a riot or something."

Spence eagerly grabbed his friend's coat sleeve and hung on so he would not be lost in the jumble of people they kept bumping up against in their exit. He was surprised when he felt Lori link her arm through his. But he tightened his grip on her, imagining she did not want to get lost either. Eventually finding themselves outside, they all took exaggerated gulps of the refreshing, cold night air and laughed.

"How long does it take for this pounding to go away?" Spence asked as he rubbed his chest.

"No kidding!" Mike agreed. "Now I know what they mean when they say 'It's not the heat, it's the humanity.' "

❧

Spence pulled his key out of the doorknob as Mike barged in ahead of him. There was a faint smell of Lysol and potpourri. Corinne had been here. He breathed a slight sigh of relief to know his apartment would at least look presentable to his guests. Although Spence was sure Mike had seen it at its worst, for some reason it was important to him that Lori liked his modest little flat.

There was a muffled exclamation as he heard the bumbled shuffling of Mike against an end table. "Spence, where are your lamps, anyway?"

"I imagine they're on the tables, unless Corinne moved them," he answered, laughing. His arm was suddenly cool. He felt Lori pull away and wondered why she had retreated so after having her arm linked through his since they had left the Blue Heron. What's more, Spence found himself missing that warmth.

He heard Mike finally flipping the switch on one of the lamps.

"Nice place," Lori said softly. "It definitely has a woman's touch."

Spence heard a slight stiffness in her tone as he headed into the kitchenette and proceeded to pull out several plates and glasses, placing them on the small, round table.

"Yeah, I don't have much time or patience to fiddle with decorating, and Corinne gets a kick out of it." He smiled at the memory of his sister's babbling while she stenciled a border around his kitchen. He had been sitting at the table trying to compose a song but had eventually given in to her cheerful chattering. He enjoyed her visits, and she always had news from college to tell him.

After everyone had found a chair, Mike and Lori began idle chitchat as they delved into the food in front of them. Spence quietly bowed his head, offering his silent prayer, then raised his head in amusement at the sudden stillness surrounding him. He nonchalantly took a handful of french fries. "So, Lori, you planning on being in the musical?"

She cleared her throat before answering. "Um, yeah, I guess so."

"Good." The little exchange seemed to break the ice all over again, and soon the three were discussing plays and the latest gossip of the theater family and chuckling over the blunders made in rehearsals and even in some of the not-so-memorable performances.

"Why do you always wear those sunglasses?" Lori asked out of the blue. "Are your eyes sensitive to the light or something?"

Mike nearly choked in surprise, but Spence ignored him, answering good-naturedly, "Yeah, I guess you could say that."

She seemed to buy the explanation. Mike frowned, wondering why Spence just didn't tell her. He couldn't think of any good reason not to—everyone else knew. But he didn't take any action to correct her misconception.

Several hours and too many bad, late-night movies later, the arm chair squeaked in protest as Mike got up. "Well, I'd better get going. It's already way past midnight. I can drop you home, Lori."

Spence took a deep breath as Lori's arm brushed against his. She had chosen the position right next to him on the couch despite the fact that there were plenty of other options for seating.

"Maybe Spence can take me home," she replied softly.

Mike coughed several times, obviously waiting for Spence to intervene.

"What?" Lori asked. "Would that cause problems with Corinne?"

"No," Spence answered, somewhat confused by her train of thought.

"Corinne's his sister," Mike stated bluntly.

Spence felt his face flush hotly. Of course. It had not even occurred to him that Lori had thought Corinne might be his—

"So what's the problem?" Lori asked.

She surely was insistent. "Well, I'd love to, Lori, but I don't have a car. I'm afraid I depend on the good old busing system for my transportation."

"I see." Her tone showed a hint of disappointment. "I'll get my coat." She slowly rose from her place beside him, and Spence followed to let his guests out.

"Thanks for the supper, Mike. My treat next time."

"Sure, no problem."

Spence knew his friend was stifling a laugh at his expense, but he chose to ignore it. Could he help it if Lori had misconstrued things?

He heard her light footsteps and the sound of her arms sliding along the nylon lining of her coat sleeves.

"Okay, Mike, let's go."

"Good night, Lori."

Her lack of response surprised Spence. It seemed a small thing to get upset over. He closed the door behind the two and returned to the couch, where he flopped down with a sigh. Taking off his glasses at last, he rubbed his eyes. The area still held the faintest aroma of Lori's perfume, and he could almost feel the soft silkiness of her long hair, brushing against his arm.

Slapping his thighs in disgust, he jumped up from the couch and headed straight to his bedroom. What was wrong with him, anyway? He had known this girl for only a few hours! Besides, he already knew what Mike had told him about her. He smirked at his own vanity, to think any woman would be interested in him. Remembering the argument that had ensued between her and Gary, he surmised the probable reason for her friendliness.

Tearing off his clothes as he went, Spence stomped toward his bed, strangely disturbed by the whole situation. He had been so used to being alone that her company had been welcome. . .pleasant. . .no matter what her motive.

God, what do I do? He stared into the never-ending blackness, waiting for some kind of answer. When none came, he rolled over and punched the defenseless fluff in his pillow. Maybe he had just been away from people too long. Maybe after being back at the theater for a while, his emotions would straighten out. Maybe. . . . He thought back to the evening's conversation and the twinkling of her airy laugh, her artistic flair when discussing set ideas, her obvious vast knowledge of the theater and many playwrights. Maybe she was different from what Mike had said. Maybe she had changed.

He gave himself an inward slap of reality as the conversation between Lori and Gary came crashing back into his mind: *Why don't you just come out and say it? You've found a new toy to play with.*

Spence laughed bitterly at the memory. "Okay, Lord. You've got some work to do on me yet. Just give me the patience to go where *You* might lead. I'll never be able to 'see' well enough to go it alone."

❧

Lori dropped to her knees, dipping her brush into the bucket and trying to get the last drop of paint. She let out a long breath as she slapped the generic white color onto the flat. There. . .that one was done. Glancing at her watch, she rolled her eyes. It was only ten o'clock.

After a restless night, she had finally gotten out of bed early and decided to head down to the theater to help with the new set construction. To her surprise, no one was there. It was then she remembered last evening's cast party. If things had gone as they usually did at those end-of-the-performance parties, nobody would be out of bed at all today. It gave her an unfamiliar satisfaction that she was not part of that crowd for once. But then, Lori grimly reminded herself, last night had not gone so well, either.

She frowned as she began the task of cleaning off her brush, trying to figure out this Spencer Berg. Why had he been eager to be rid of her? Well, maybe not eager. . .he had almost seemed afraid of her. Afraid to have anything to do with her. She smiled at the thought, wondering how the great Spencer Berg could be afraid of anything. He and those silly glasses of his. She wondered what color his eyes were behind the blackness of those mysterious shades.

The side stage door opened and Lori glanced up, surprised. She swallowed the lump in her throat as she saw Gary coming toward her. Turning her attention back to the task at hand, she quickly began swishing the bristles in the potent-smelling turpentine. Oddly enough, Gary marched right on by, continuing toward the men's dressing room. Lori let out a shaky breath and calmly stood up, wiping her hands on a rag.

The same door swung open again, and she turned to see a girl standing in the doorway, glancing from side to side. She seemed lost. "Can I help you?" Lori asked.

The girl shrugged her small shoulders and started to open her mouth to respond.

"Thanks, darlin'." Gary's voice made Lori blanch. He came up behind her, his breath tickling her ear, speaking loud enough for her alone to hear. "She knows all she needs to."

Lori whirled around, ready to give him another dose of what she had started last night, but he intercepted her arm before it reached his face.

"What's the matter, love?" His narrowed eyes mocked her. "Does the truth hurt?"

She stood speechless, shaking with rage. "Go away," she whispered venomously.

"Gladly." With a sneer he headed toward his bubbly blond companion.

Lori managed to hold her ground, standing ramrod straight until they had left the premises. It was then that she collapsed to the stage, letting Gary's words fully encompass her in all their stinging truth. Strangely, her eyes remained dry as the sobs got lost in her heaving chest. She studied the cracks in the stage floor, trying to remember the last time she had cried.

Hearing the door opening again, Lori scurried to find an escape. The last thing she needed was to have Gary gloating over her weakness. Scrambling to the edge of the stage floor, she dropped into the orchestra pit and squeezed into the oversized cubbyhole that still held the subtle scent of valve oil. The musicians usually kept their instruments here, but fortunately, most of them had taken theirs home after last night's closing performance.

Nestling snugly against the back wall in the covering darkness, she listened to the two voices approaching and caught her breath when she recognized one as Spence's. The other voice, a young woman's, she could not place.

"You sure you're okay here?"

"Yes, Mom!" Spence laughed at the young woman's question. "I practically live here, remember?"

"Lived here," she corrected him.

Papers shuffled and a few piano keys plunked before the woman's voice came again. "Spence, I just—"

"Goodbye, Corinne." Spence squelched any further comments by beginning a loud Brahms rhapsody.

Lori figured Spence's sister had finally left when he ceased playing and began whistling instead. She heard him sifting papers again, and she craned her neck around the short wall to try and see what he was doing.

The piano opened into a sweet, ballad-type introduction that captivated her. Eagerly anticipating the entrance where the vocals should come in, she closed her eyes, curiously waiting for his much-acclaimed singing voice. The music halted and her eyes flew open with the silence.

Spence started over with the same melody and again stopped, although this time he hummed along, his lone voice resonating in the vast emptiness of the large auditorium.

Not able to stand it any longer, Lori stealthily moved to the outer edge of her little shell, hoping she would not be seen. She was not sure how Spence would take it, knowing she was more or less spying on him. Besides, she was rather enjoying her secretiveness.

Easing out farther, she could see his face plainly between the soundboard and the lid of the baby grand. She grinned at her good fortune. He was not wearing his glasses! Her stomach began to flutter as she realized she was about to find out what his eyes looked like.

She squinted, straining ever so slightly forward. She could not really tell from this distance. They looked dark. . .well, no, maybe gray. She frowned in her concentration.

A slew of sheet music fell from the piano, fluttering to the floor in disarray. Lori jumped back into her hiding space as Spence halted his playing again with a heavy sigh. She heard him pushing back the bench, and she peeked around the corner cautiously. He had dropped to his hands and knees and was pushing the strewn papers toward him.

Something about the whole scene struck Lori as odd. She cocked her head in thought and then sucked in a gasp as she realized what he was doing. . .or rather, what he was not doing. He was not *looking* for his papers, he was *feeling* for them. His head did not even drop once, and in his now-upturned face, she saw clearly the cloudy patches that marred his dark eyes.

three

Lori bit her lower lip as her brows knitted together in confusion. *Well, you're pretty quick, aren't you, Miss Sommers?* she mocked herself. She stood, helpless and hidden, wondering what to do. He looked so pitiful down there, scrounging around on his hands and knees.

Throwing all caution, and what she considered good sense, to the wind, she quietly made her way to his side. Kneeling beside him, she made short work of what was left of his pile of scattered papers. They worked in silence, which she thought somewhat strange. He had not even reacted to her sudden presence.

When the last paper was in place, Spence tapped them neatly against the floor and returned them to their rightful place on the piano. Lori stood, chewing her thumbnail, afraid to look at him even though she knew he could not see her.

His quiet voice finally broke the line of heavy silence. "Thank you."

Lori nodded then, realizing her action could not be seen, uttered a meek, "You're welcome."

Because of Spence's lack of reaction, it was obvious to Lori that he had been aware of her presence the whole time. There was no other explanation for his calmness. Waiting until he had seated himself back on the bench, she finally ventured to ask, "How did you know I was here?"

"Smell," he replied, never looking up from the keys where his long fingers had started to coax out a soft melody.

"Smell?" she asked, almost insulted.

She watched his mouth curl up into a whimsical smile. "I

smelled the paint and turpentine when I first got here," he admitted, "and I smelled your perfume when I came into the pit."

"My perfume?"

"When you can't see, the other senses sort of take over." He smiled at her openly now, his face toward hers. "Besides, I remembered your perfume from last night. It's nice, by the way. What is it?"

Her face grew uncomfortably warm. "Provocative." She wondered why she should be embarrassed about the name of a silly fragrance.

"It certainly is." He grinned while he shot his eyebrows up and down.

Clearing her throat, Lori shifted her weight from one foot to the other, wondering what to do. Maybe it would be best if she just left.

"Care to join me?" Spence asked, sliding over several inches on the wide bench.

Shrugging her shoulders, she complied. "Why not?"

They sat mutely, their sides brushing together, as he leaned into the keys, putting his entire body into the emotion of the sad serenade. Lori recognized it immediately as one of Beethoven's works. She watched in utter fascination at the deft movements of his long, nimble fingers stroking the keys in turn. He truly was talented. How can he still do this when he cannot see?

"Why didn't you tell me you were blind?" she asked bluntly.

The rhythm of the melody never faltered as he answered her. "I thought you knew. That someone had told you."

She did not buy that for a minute. "Even after I asked you why you wore those glasses? And after I asked you to take me home?"

He suddenly seemed uncomfortable and he stopped playing. Shaking his head, he kept his face down at the long row of ivory keys. "I don't know," he admitted. "I don't know why I didn't tell you." He paused, as if trying to find a reason for her. "I guess you were the first person I'd encountered in a long time who didn't realize it. It was kind of fun to be in the land of the seeing one more time."

"At my expense?" She knew her voice betrayed the hint of annoyance she felt. It irked her to think he had probably enjoyed his little game with her.

"Well," Spence turned his face to hers, "what would you have done if I had taken you home?"

Now it was her turn to squirm in discomfort. How many times had she asked herself that question the night before?

She glanced up and found herself looking into the cloudy chasms of his eyes, which she now discovered were a very dark brown. They looked blankly at her, but she knew that behind their dim façade was an overwhelming kindness she could not understand.

To her relief, he turned back to the keyboard once again, not really waiting for an answer to his question. Maybe he had thrown it out just for her to ponder. Well, she was not willing to do that right now. . .if ever.

Lori eagerly headed the conversation onto another avenue. "What song was that you were playing before?"

"This one?" He picked up the same intro that had caught her attention earlier. "That's the song I'm in the process of perfecting. I'm trying to get a contract with a recording company."

"To sing?"

"Well, actually to write. I enjoy singing well enough, but my heart is here." He pointed to the keys before him and then to the stack of papers she had helped him pick up.

She casually took one and noticed the raised lines of the staff. "You can find your way around on these just by touch?"

He laughed at her astonishment. "If you knew how long

I've been tinkering at writing down music, it wouldn't surprise you. But I do carry this along, too." He patted a pocket tape recorder on top of the piano that she had missed seeing before. "Besides, companies today want people with a little character to their voice. Something to set them apart from the rest. I'm afraid I'm stuck with my painfully correct choirboy tenor."

"Sing for me," she said excitedly as she repositioned herself on the hard bench.

"Really?" He sounded surprised.

"Yes, really."

Shrugging his shoulders, he started into an upbeat tempo, then stopped abruptly.

"What?" she asked, frowning.

"On one condition." He grinned at her slyly. "You join me for lunch."

"For lunch? Okay, whatever." She settled back and waited for him to finish the song.

"And, please, try to contain your excitement."

Lori flushed as she realized she had hurt his feelings with her lack of enthusiasm. But he did not give her time to apologize. Instead, he started up the jovial tune again, and she had to laugh aloud when she began to recognize Stephen Foster's melody, "Camptown Races."

"Join me," he threw at her before the first line approached. "De Camptown ladies sing dis song, doo-dah! doo-dah!"

Lori tried to control her giggling as Spence belted out the ridiculous lyrics in a heavy bass voice, but she could not stop. She could not remember when she had laughed so hard.

Spence seemed to enjoy the effect he was having on her and began throwing in twisted, contorted faces as he changed his accent from heavy German, to deep southern, to several other accents she could not even label.

No one had ever tried this hard to make her laugh. . .to

make her happy, period. Slowly, her chuckle died. First a date to lunch, now this. . . . What did he want from her, anyway?

Much too involved in his merrymaking, Spence went on and on with his antics as Lori pulled away and stood up from the bench, studying him carefully. She did not quite know how to take this sort of behavior.

Spence stopped playing and turned in her direction. "What's the matter? Stephen Foster not one of your favorite song writers?"

The frown she felt creasing her brow intensified. "What are you doing?"

"What am I doing? Well, I'm sitting here, playing the piano. What are you doing?"

Lori squashed the emotions that were wreaking havoc in her already mixed-up heart. She tried to laugh lightly, hoping she would fool him. "Quite an actress, aren't I? Just trying out the moody side. Always practicing, you know. . . ." She chuckled half-heartedly when she realized she was babbling.

He hesitated before nodding, and she grimaced, knowing he had not bought it. "So, when's lunch?" she said, rerouting the conversation once again. She seemed to be resorting to that a lot lately.

Spence let out a long breath. "I guess we could go now."

"Sounds good," she said, a little too enthusiastically. "Where are we going?" She helped grab up his papers and tape recorder.

"Well, I thought we'd go to Lake of the Isles, if you don't mind."

"A picnic? Are you crazy? It's freezing!" Pulling on her heavy, leather jacket reminded her of that fact.

"It's in the fifties today," he argued. "The snow's all gone."

"How about somewhere warmer?" Lori appealed.

"Bahamas?"

"Florida?" she shot back.

"Okay, I give. You choose a spot."

"Okay, let's meet at. . .my place."

Spence seemed surprised at her suggestion, and she began to wonder if it was a bad idea to invite him there. She was about to open her mouth and tell him to pick the place, but he cut her off. "All right. I don't know where you live, though."

"Oh, I brought my car today. You can come with me."

"Hmmm," he mused. "A break from the bus, what a treat."

"Well," she laughed, "you may not think so after my driving."

"Lead the way." Spence swung his arm out ahead of him.

Lori stepped out in front of him and then stopped abruptly, causing him to collide into her back.

"I see what you mean," he said, smiling. "A pileup already, and we haven't even left the building."

"I was just wondering if. . .well, do you need—"

"I can manage okay until we get outside, then I'll need your arm."

Lori sighed in relief at his ability to conduct himself in awkward moments. As she trudged toward the theater's side door, she wished she possessed that gift.

Shutting the car door on her smiling passenger, Lori felt serious doubts creep into her mind about this whole lunch date. What had she been thinking when she had invited him to her home? Rounding the front of her bright red sports car, she chided herself, knowing full well what she should expect.

It was always the same, wasn't it? Strangely enough, she found herself drawn to this guy. The only thing that made her a little uneasy was something she could not quite put her finger on. Something about him that was strong, confident. . .yet quiet.

Well, she decided smartly, that was why they were headed to her turf. Being on her home stage ought to take away that edge Spence seemed to have over her.

Slipping her car into first gear, she smiled to herself. She was in charge now. And that's the way it had to be.

❧

Spence tightened his grip on the door handle beside him as Lori squealed the tires leaving the parking lot. His eyebrows raised in surprise and uncertainty as she maneuvered the quick little car toward wherever they were headed.

"Nice car," he said, trying to make conversation light while his fingers tightened on the molded plastic handle.

"Thanks. It's a restored Stingray."

"Is the theater paying better than I remember?"

"Hardly," she answered. "This was a gift."

"Really?"

"From my dad, in case you're wondering," she added.

"Oh." Spence wondered what her father did for a living.

They had not driven more than a few miles when he sensed the darkness of pulling into some type of garage or parking ramp, judging from the echo of the car's humming motor within the enclosed walls.

"So, where are we, anyway?" he asked as he opened his door and uncoiled his long legs from the front seat.

"Manor Suites." He heard her locking the doors and coming to his side to offer her arm.

He let out a low whistle as she led him along. "A Manor Suites condo, a classic sports car. . . Is all this from Daddy?"

"Yes."

Her answer was curt, but he was not dissuaded from continuing. "Where do your parents live, anyway?"

"I'm originally from Florida." Another brief answer.

Spence felt her pull him into an elevator. She punched a series of buttons he knew to be an access code for an establishment like Manor Suites. Security here was top-notch. It had to be with the kind of wealth that the people who lived here had. He tried again to find out some background on this mystery woman. "So what does your father do?"

Lori sighed with impatience. "He's in politics."

"Ah, our tax dollars at work," he kidded. When no reply came, he cleared his throat and tried again. "So, what made him let his little girl run all the way up here to Minneapolis?"

The elevator doors slid open and she stepped into the hall, pulling him with her. He heard her fumbling with her keys and then heard a stifled exclamation as the keys hit the carpet below them. She jiggled them in the lock once more and, taking his elbow, led him to her couch where he felt himself being almost shoved down. It did not take long to figure out that he had touched a nerve.

"If you'll excuse me, I'm going to change out of my paint-spattered clothes."

Spence turned in his seat toward the hard voice and nodded. Her retreating footsteps slowed momentarily. "And I would rather not discuss my father anymore."

With a shiver from her icy tone, he gave a solemn nod he was not sure she saw and twisted back around on the sofa. *Well,* he thought, *this should be an interesting lunch.* At least he now knew what *not* to talk about.

It really was not any of his business, anyway. But Spence could not shake the uncomfortable tugging at his heart about what had made Lori so cold toward this mystery father of hers.

four

"Well," Lori's voice came from behind Spence once again. "I hope I have something decent to feed you."

She sounded more relaxed.

"Okay."

The refrigerator door opened and he heard her rummaging through its contents. "Chicken salad on croissants okay? I don't have as much as I thought. Guess it's time for a grocery shopping trip."

"That'll do just fine." Spence stood up and started to head toward the kitchen but thought better of it and sat back down. The last thing he needed was to trip over something and make a bumbling fool of himself.

She must have noticed his gesture, for she was promptly at his side, leading him toward the dining table.

"Thanks." He smiled warmly at her. "I really didn't want to get into a wrestling match with any of your furniture."

"Good thing," she laughed. "Most of it's glass."

Spence took his seat and waited while Lori prepared their lunch.

"Speaking of grocery shopping," she commented, "how do you do that?"

"Oh. Well, you know those bar codes they put on most of the items?"

"Um-hm."

"They have a dual purpose, really. Next time you go shopping, pick one up and feel it. You'll notice it's raised a tiny bit. We can read the contents by feeling the bar codes."

There were several seconds of silence before her teasing

voice returned. “Really? You know what, Spencer Berg. I think you’re lying.”

Grinning, he shrugged his shoulders. “Some people buy it.”

“Raised bar codes,” she scoffed.

He heard her sliding a plate in front of him and then the sound of Lori crunching into her own sandwich. He waited, wondering how to go about this delicately.

“So, what do we have here?” He hoped she would take the hint from that.

“Um, there’s a chicken salad croissant, some chips, and I managed to dig up a few carrot sticks.”

“Sounds good.” He paused again.

“What’s the matter?” she asked. “Oh, I forgot. . .you like to um, pray, don’t you? Well, go ahead. I don’t mind.”

“Thanks.” He bowed his head and offered up his silent prayer. When he had finished, he was still stuck in the same situation. “Uh, Lori?”

“Yeah?”

“I kind of need some help here.” He felt a touch foolish, though he was not sure why. He had had to do this before. She did not respond audibly, and he was beginning to wonder if she thought she might have to spoon-feed him. “If you could just give me the coordinates of my food in relation to a clock, it would help keep me from feeding your floor.”

“A clock?” The poor woman sounded thoroughly perplexed.

“Yeah, like sandwich at noon, carrots at five, and so on.”

“Ohhh. Let’s see, your sandwich is at. . .two; your chips are at. . .ten; and your carrots are at six. Is that okay?”

“That’s perfect.” He let out a long breath as he confidently reached for a carrot stick. “So, Lori,” Spence changed the subject, “how long have you taken voice lessons?”

“Lessons?” She spoke around a partially full mouth. “I’ve never taken any lessons.”

“Really?” he asked, incredulous. “None at all? No coaching

or anything?"

"No. You sound surprised."

"I am." He nodded. "You have a fabulous voice and your control is astounding. It's rare to find that quality in an untrained voice. God has certainly blessed you with a gift."

"But I was born with this voice," Lori retorted.

Spence pursed his lips together, trying to contain the laughter that wanted to jump out. She almost sounded offended at his comment. He let his inner laughter manifest itself in a smile. "You know what? I like you, Lori."

"Thanks." Her own smile was evident in her tone.

It disappointed but did not surprise him that Lori did not return the compliment. For some reason, he got the feeling she had been told that a lot.

❧

"So," Erica giggled as she snapped open her soft drink can. "What's he like?"

Lori settled next to her friend on the sectional sofa. "What do you mean? You've known him for longer than I have!"

Erica's wide, brown eyes rolled in impatience. "Oh, sure. At the theater. Big deal." She scooted closer to Lori, giddy with anticipation. "Come on, Lori, 'fess up! He was here, wasn't he? What happened?"

Lori turned a critical eye toward her visitor. "Well, first I made him lunch. Then, we sat on the couch here and talked. Then. . . ." Her voice tapered off suggestively.

"What? What?" Erica bounced up and down before she realized she was spilling cola on the white upholstery. She swiped at the spots with a nearby napkin, her eyes never leaving Lori's face.

"Then. . .I took him home." Lori had to laugh when her friend's face fell.

"So what happened there?" Erica seemed sure there had to be more to the story.

"Sorry," Lori apologized over her shoulder as she went to retrieve a rag to wipe up the spill properly.

When she returned, Erica was shaking her head. "I can't believe it."

"What did you guys say you called him?" Lori asked, blotting the cushion gently.

"The Ice Berg."

"Yeah." She nodded. "That about covers it."

"Oh, well," Erica sighed, twisting her finger around one of her black ringlets, "maybe it just takes time."

"I don't think so." Lori stood up. "There's something different about him."

"Oh, that," her friend snorted as she jumped up to toss her can in the garbage. "Well, he's religious, you know."

"Really?" Lori tucked that new piece of information away.

Erica grabbed her jacket from the arm of the sofa. "He and Maggie go to the same church, I think. Well, I'd better go. Thanks for the visit. And I'm sorry."

"That's all right. The stain came out right away."

"I meant with Spence."

Lori locked her gaze on Erica, not knowing what to say. Her friend looked equally uncomfortable before heading toward the door and waving a cheery goodbye as she pulled it closed behind her.

As Lori turned back to her kitchen, it suddenly hit her that Erica was most likely speaking with regret because at some time, she had failed to uncover the secrets of Spencer Berg as well! The thought that Erica might be interested in him churned Lori's insides in an inexplicable fashion. Why should she care? But then she smiled, feeling a measure of smug satisfaction in the fact that Erica *had* failed.

❧

"Good service." Maggie squeezed Spence's arm affectionately. "I could listen to you sing those old hymns all day."

"Thanks, Maggie." Spence gave her hand a firm pat. "I thought Pastor Schell's sermon was really good tonight. I guess a lot of singles need to be reminded of the whole idea of being unequally yoked with a nonbeliever. It can be so easy to let emotions sway us." The slightest discomfort had pricked Spence's conscience during the sermon, and he knew that a certain young actress was the reason.

"I know," Maggie answered solemnly. "I'm just so thankful that my Patrick was a believer. It makes it easier knowing I'll see him again one day, too."

"I'll bet he was a great guy." Spence gave her a soft smile. "So," he said, changing the subject, "you all set for the new production tomorrow?"

"Ready as ever. I always enjoy the musicals so."

Spence shuffled his feet on the tiled floor. He guessed now was as good a time as any. "Say," he hedged, "do you come into contact with Lori Sommers very often?"

"Oh, yes. A sweet, sweet girl." Maggie sounded sincere enough.

"I see. Has she ever—"

"Excuse me, Mr. Berg?" a quiet, girlish voice came from beside Spence.

"Yes?" He turned toward her.

"I was told that you were employed at the Penny Lane Theater."

"Sure am. What can I do for you?" He pushed his sunglasses up the bridge of his nose.

"Well," she said nervously, "I was wondering if you'll be starting a new production any time soon. I'd really like to try out."

"As a matter of fact, we're holding auditions tomorrow for a musical. What's your name?"

"I'm Diane Richards." She pressed a small hand into his, shaking it timidly.

Spence wondered if she had the courage to try out for anything.

"Come on down, Diane. Tomorrow at about ten o'clock. By the way, have you been attending Abundant Life Fellowship for long?"

"This is my third week. I really like it. God just seems so evident in the people here."

"Yeah, we feel that way, too. It'll sure be nice to have another Christian down at the theater, eh, Maggie?" Spence nudged a shoulder toward the older woman.

"It certainly will. I'm Maggie Dempsey, Diane. Makeup, hair, costumes, and wherever else they can squeeze me in," she chortled in her usual jovial fashion.

Spence stifled a yawn. "Sorry." He smiled. "By the end of Sunday evening service, I'm pretty well shot. But come tomorrow, Diane, you'll see me more awake. . .I hope."

He was rewarded with a quiet laugh, and the three said their goodbyes.

As Spence boarded the bus toward home, he thought about the new woman at church. She seemed sweet and had vaguely reminded him of his own sister, Corinne. It would be fun to have some new blood at the tryouts.

The subject of the tryouts brought back thoughts of Lori. He felt a twinge of regret over the interruption to his question about her. There were a few things about her that confused him, in particular, her demeanor. It could change so suddenly. Maybe it was just one of her idiosyncrasies. Everyone had them. But deep down, he did not think that was the reason.

❧

"Okay, Spence, this is your baby. Take her over." Tom, the stage manager, pressed the microphone into Spence's hand.

"Hey, guys," Spence turned toward the crowd he knew was seated on the stage floor. "Well, as you've probably heard, we're opting for a Gene Kelly classic this summer for our musical. We've kind of taken an informal poll among you and *Brigadoon* seemed to win out. So, tryouts will be today, and rehearsals start Wednesday."

A collective groan rose up from the group.

Spence grinned. "Nope. No rest for you, now that I'm back. So, if you all want to take a seat," he motioned behind himself to the auditorium, "we'll start the process here."

Spence headed down the side steps and found his way to the piano. He preferred to sit at the instrument, since it was where he would be during performances.

He was about to tell Mike to gear up the tape machine when thundering footsteps clambered up the steps to the stage. Spence did not have to guess twice as to what was going on. "Gary, Erica, please get off the stage, and we'll do this in a somewhat orderly fashion."

It was the same at every production. . .the two most aggressive actors in the group, vying for the number one spot. Childish, yes, but he had to chuckle. At least they were eager.

"Okay," Spence took control again. "Let's be methodical about this and start the auditions alphabetically."

A good hour into the tryouts, Spence was pleased with the results. A lot of people had improved markedly during the last year. This would be a quality musical.

Diane Richards pulled off her song in a breathy soprano with minimal nervous mistakes. She showed promise but needed experience. He would start her out in the chorus this year, but she would be an asset to the group.

When it was Lori's turn to audition, Spence held his breath in anticipation. He knew she would be trying for the lead part of Fiona Campbell, and there were no doubts in his mind that she would get it. It would be hard to surpass her strong soprano. He was relieved that Diane was done and did not have to try and follow an act like Lori's. It could be disheartening to someone just starting out.

Several voices threw encouraging comments up to Lori, and Spence smiled at the homey, familiar atmosphere that seemed to pervade everything that went on here at Penny Lane.

" 'Waitin' For My Dearie,' " she informed Mike, who was heading up the tape machine with all the show tunes.

"Yeah, I'll bet you're a waitin'!" Gary sneered from his seat with the others.

There were muffled titters among the crew, and Spence felt himself blushing for Lori. He wished he could see her face, for there was no audible reaction from the stage.

"Go ahead, Lori," he urged her as he motioned for Mike to start the tape. Acknowledging Gary's crude comment was the last thing that buffoon needed. He might take it as a sign of encouragement.

If Lori was at all disturbed by the exchange, it certainly did not show in her voice. She carried the song beautifully, and Spence felt the goose bumps traveling up his arms. *Man, but this girl can sing!*

He recalled the conversation they had had over lunch. Her lack of professional voice training still shocked him. It was just so unusual to come across a voice of her caliber that had not been coached.

He still found himself pondering over her reaction to his comment about her God-given gift. Her answer was so innocent, it could have just as easily come from a little girl. But then, he realized, there seemed to be a lot of subtle things like that about Lori, despite her façade of sophistication. Not that he doubted what Mike had informed him about her, but there was indeed an innocence there. Almost like a little girl who was lost.

After going through the entire company, the day was pretty well spent. Confident he had all the parts decided, Spence let out his breath in a whoosh, raking his fingers through his hair.

"Long day, huh?"

Spence heard Mike plop down on the piano bench that he had just vacated. "Yeah, I guess I'm not used to the long hours yet."

"You got the parts doled out?" Mike plunked out a simple tune on the keys.

"Yeah, I think so. I'm really pleased with a lot of the people. They've really improved. Some fresh talent, too." Spence remembered there had been several new people on stage besides Diane.

He started to shove his small tape recorder into the zippered pocket of his windbreaker. There was an unusually long silence, especially considering how talkative Mike normally was. "Something the matter?"

"I'm not sure."

Spence slipped onto the bench next to his friend and played the beginning chords of "Chopsticks." He had to smile when Mike chimed in with the upper notes. That was about the extent of Mike's piano repertoire, but the two of them always had fun with it.

The small diversion had the effect on Mike that Spence had hoped. His tension eased considerably as they laughed over their duet.

"So," Spence started, "what's up?"

Mike let out a long sigh. "Well, I heard you were at Lori's a few days ago."

"Yeah. We had lunch." Spence felt some of the earlier awkwardness creeping back into the conversation.

"I guess you know what you're doing." The comment came out more like a question.

"Yes, I know what I'm doing," Spence reassured him.

Mike was quiet again for a time, as if he were choosing his words carefully. "Just be careful, buddy."

Spence almost snickered at the ridiculousness of his friend's statement. What would he have to fear from a little wisp of a woman like Lori? But he held his amusement back, realizing Mike was deadly serious.

"Okay, I will. But I don't see—"

"Hi, guys." Lori's voice came across the stage as she neared the pit.

"I gotta go." Mike stood up and placed a firm hand on Spence's shoulder. "Remember what I said."

Spence nodded as his friend's hand pulled away.

"See ya later, Lori."

"Bye, Mike."

Spence felt Lori squeeze beside him, and he inwardly chastised the quickening of his heartbeat. All of a sudden, Mike's advice did not seem so silly. Maybe he had better be careful.

"Whatcha doin'?" she asked in a quiet voice.

"I was just going to head home."

"You busy?"

"Not really, why?"

"I thought maybe we could try dinner together." She sounded more enthusiastic about this prospective date than the last one.

"Sure." He stopped to think a moment. "How about the Imperial Palace? You like Chinese?"

"Oh. I thought maybe we could have dinner at my place again."

Oh, boy. He'd have to tread carefully here. "Well, it's my turn and I'm a lousy cook, so how about we just meet there at say. . .seven?" There, that did not leave her any room to argue with him.

"Okay," Lori answered hesitatingly. "But I could drive."

"Please," he said, grimacing. "You're bruising my ego, already."

She finally laughed. "Okay, seven o'clock. If I get there early," she added, "I'll be the one in the red dress."

"Oh, thanks!" he called after her retreating back. Spence smiled in anticipation. He really enjoyed her company. Tonight would be fun, he assured himself. Then why couldn't he get Mike's concerned voice out of his mind?

five

Lori fastened a gold belt around her red silk dress and smoothed the billowy folds of the trumpet skirt. Crossing to her brass vanity, she sat down on the cushioned bench. She pulled a strand of wispy, honey blonde hair through her fingers, wishing that it had more life to it. Sighing, she added a touch of mascara to the light lashes around her eyes. She could never decide if they were blue or green; they seemed to change with what she wore.

To finish up, she applied a hint of blush to her cheeks and decided to forego the lipstick. She usually didn't wear it anyway. In fact, she rarely wore makeup. Most people told her she did not need it, and she got so tired of all the thick makeup from the theater that it was a treat to let her skin breathe for a change.

Lori took one last look at herself and sputtered into a laugh. Why was she so concerned about her appearance? Spence could not see her, anyway! Shrugging her shoulders, she turned to leave, noticing it was nearly quarter to seven. At the last minute, she spun around and grabbed a small atomizer from her table. She misted some of the fragrance on her neck, remembering how Spence had commented on the perfume before. Grinning as she tossed her keys into the air, she hoped that tonight he would find her exactly that. . .provocative.

A few minutes later, Lori pulled her Stingray into an empty parking spot and hurried to the pillared entrance of the restaurant. Wonderful smells of stir fry and spices wafted out to greet her as she pulled open the heavy door. There was quite a crowd already, and she hoped Spence had made reservations.

A smiling Chinese woman approached her, and Lori started to ask about a party by the name of Berg when she caught sight of Spence's dark head and sunglasses across the room. Pointing in his direction, she thanked the woman and started toward the cozy corner booth.

She slid into the seat across from him and clutched his hands that were busily scribbling down something on a napkin.

"Hi."

He lifted his head and gave her a huge grin. A dimple appeared in his right cheek and Lori wondered how she had missed seeing it before. It was so charming, like most everything else about him, she mused. Glancing down at the napkin, she noticed several chord notations and some jottings of words, barely intelligible. "How is that going to help you?" she laughed.

A sheepish smile crossed his face. "Just can't stop, can I? Once a songwriter, always a songwriter. Either Mike or Corinne will reread this back to me later, although I can usually remember what I've written. Just the process of putting it down on paper helps a lot."

Lori smiled gently. He was so different from anyone else she had known. Quiet, yet confident. And there was that something else she had yet to put her finger on.

She noticed that he, too, had taken a reprieve from his usual jeans and sweat shirts. He wore a white, dress shirt and a thin, black tie with piano keys running up the length of it.

"Nice tie." She bit her lip in a smirk.

"Oh," he chuckled. "My mom gave this to me."

"She must have a sense of humor."

"She does. My dad, too." He looked contemplative for a minute.

A waiter placed a pot of tea and two cups, along with menus, on their table and promised to be back shortly to take their order.

"Where does your family live?" Lori picked up the topic again, hoping it would keep the conversation away from her.

"I'm from Duluth. My parents still live there, as do my older sister and brother and their families. Corinne goes to the university here."

"Big family." She raised her eyebrows in surprise.

"Just four of us. Not so big. How about you? Any siblings?"

Lori felt her throat tighten. She debated whether to make up some fantastic story about an idyllic family or just be honest and hope Spence would not pry any further. She decided on the latter. "No," she replied curtly and released a huge sigh of relief when the waiter returned.

After they had placed their orders, she jumped on the chance to start another topic. "You realize I know very little about you. For as much as everyone talks about you, there's not much to it."

"Fire away." He grinned. "I'm fair game to any question except what I was doing the night my little sister's goldfish mysteriously got flushed down the toilet."

Lori wrinkled her nose as she laughed. "I'm not sure I want to hear about that. How about. . .do you like any kind of music other than the rag and jazz tunes you're always plunking out?"

"Oh, certainly. But baroque comes off much better on violins than it does on a piano."

"You like baroque?"

"Love it. Purcell and Vivaldi are the best."

Lori could not have been more pleased. Topic after topic, they seemed to have very similar tastes. This dinner was going much better than she had expected.

Thankfully, Spence did not broach the subject of her family again. She was glad he was content to just enjoy her company.

"I am stuffed." Spence leaned back against the padded seat.

"Good." Lori smiled. "That means you are in no shape to try and use public transportation. I'm taking you home."

"I don't know," he hedged.

Just then the waiter came with the bill and Spence handed him a credit card. Lori bit her lip in anticipation. Things could not fall apart now.

"So?" she asked again after the waiter had left.

"So, what?"

"Am I taking you home or not?"

He seemed to contemplate it for a while until he finally nodded his head. "Okay. I guess that would be all right."

"Good." Lori felt the smile creeping across her cheeks. Everything seemed to be going smoothly.

❧

"So," Spence ushered her into his apartment, "would you like some coffee or anything?"

"No thanks. I'm fine." He heard her clicking on one of his table lamps.

"Sorry." He gestured toward the faint light that seemed to glow from far off. "I forget that other people need light."

"How much can you see?" Her voice was soft, curious.

"Oh, just dim light really. Enough to know it's present. Otherwise nothing. No shadows or outlines." He moved to the couch and sat down in a heap, loosening his tie. "Sorry for the informality, but I hate these things! I feel like I have a noose around my neck." Emphasizing his comment, he slipped the tie through his collar and flung it haphazardly over his shoulder.

Spence heard Lori laugh as she approached him. Holding his breath, he waited until she sat down. She squeezed in next to him as though the couch were already crowded. Realizing he had expected it, he wondered why his heart was racing to beat the band.

She laced her fingers through his and spoke almost in a whisper. "Tell me about your accident."

Between the intoxicating scent of her perfume and the presence of her breathy whisper seemingly only inches from his face, Spence was not sure if he could recall anything at the moment.

"Um," he stalled. "I was working in my brother's lab, you see. . . ." Her free hand was now combing its fingers through his hair, toying with his cowlick as she brushed it away from his forehead. "I, uh, wasn't wearing goggles, like an idiot, and there was this chemical reaction in the beaker I was working over. . . ." Spence heard himself speed up, trying to get the story out before he forgot how to talk. "They, the chemicals, sprayed up into my eyes, and even though my brother helped rinse them out right away, my corneas were scarred and. . . . Able to recognize babbling when he heard it, he shut up.

There had to be something else they might be able to discuss. "Baroque!" he exclaimed as he jumped up from the couch.

Lori sighed heavily from behind him as he headed toward his CD player. Locating his Henry Purcell disk, Spence placed it into the machine and waited for the sound of the mellow strings to fill the room.

It gave him a measure of relief to be some distance away from Lori. His heart was just about back down to its normal pace when he felt her beside him.

She gently turned him toward her. "Can we just take these off?" She slid the glasses from his face.

He found himself feeling very vulnerable and exposed. Hoping his eyes were pointed in the general direction of her face, he swallowed hard. "What do you want from me, Lori?"

Her laugh was light, almost teasing. "Do we have to do this like your meal? Let's see. . .eyes are at ten and two o'clock; nose is at. . .in the middle, I guess; and my lips are right at six o'clock. . .time for dinner."

He felt her leaning closer and closer until their breath mingled together and her incredibly soft, full lips smoothed over his.

Mike's little piece of advice that had tucked itself somewhere in Spence's brain now sent off loud warning bells. He heard them. He knew why they were there. He knew what he should do. Then why did he find his arms folding around her waist, pulling her tightly to him?

"I knew it was there," Lori said hoarsely.

As if a flash had gone off in his mind, Spence pulled himself away, turned, and gripped the edge of his stereo cabinet as though it were the only thing holding him up.

"I think you'd better go," he murmured. He quickly shook his head, trying to rid it of the buzzing that reverberated through his ears.

"What?"

"I said. . . ." Spence took a fortifying breath as he shoved himself away from the heavy piece of furniture. "I think you'd better go."

Lori was much too silent. It was almost eerie.

He shifted uncomfortably, crossing his arms across his chest. Still no response. He was beginning to wonder if she was even there. Maybe she had slipped out and the crashing in his brain had prevented him from hearing it. "Lori?"

She did not answer, but he heard her walking away. He could not let the evening end on this note. Things had been going too well up until that point. Sprinting toward the door, he caught it just as her hand reached the knob. "I'm sorry if I offended you in any way—"

"Please, don't say anything," she said harshly. "I should have known better. They told me. . . ."

"Who told you what?"

"Everyone, 'Mr. Ice Berg.' I'm sorry I even bothered you." She yanked on the door with a strength that surprised Spence, but he held it closed.

"Why exactly did you come here tonight?" His voice was stern. He knew he had to get to the bottom of this.

"What do you mean?" She sounded angry and exasperated.

"You heard the question. Why this whole date tonight? Why so friendly?" He paused for a split second. "Why me?"

Another firm tug at the door.

"Come on, Lori. Let me in on this. What's going on behind the scenes?"

A sharp crack rang through his ears as her hot slap jolted him, its warm sting traveling across his cheek.

Spence faced her evenly. "Well, I guess that answers my question, doesn't it? But I hate to think I'm in the same ranks as good old Gary."

"You're not!" she hissed. "You're worse!" With that, she wrenched open the door, and he listened to her quick footsteps retreating down the hall. Spence closed the door and, with a sigh of resignation, clicked the latch, half wondering why he had even entertained thoughts of forming any kind of relationship with Lori. He had been forewarned. He should have known better.

six

Lori swallowed the lump in throat and pushed open the steel side door to the theater. The twinge she always felt upon arrival was a familiar one now. But what made it so annoying was that she knew it was from her unmended relationship with Spence.

The uneasiness had been so strong a few weeks ago that she had toyed with the idea of not returning to Penny Lane. But the more she thought about it, the more she realized how foolish it would be. She was an actress. She had a job to do. Acting was no different, whether on stage or in real life. Now she just had two roles to play. It would be a challenge.

Hiking her chin and throwing back her hair, she tromped in with new determination. She had paid her dues one too many times already, and within the last few weeks she had decided . . .no more. From now on it was she and she alone.

"Hey, Fiona, my love."

Todd Sawyer was, as always, waiting promptly in his position for the beginning scene of the rehearsal. She returned his wave and took the steps to the stage, two at a time.

"Hi yourself, Tommy." Lori grinned broadly at her leading man and, leaning over, ruffled his mop of curly brown hair.

She drew perverse satisfaction from the fact that Todd had been given the part over Gary. At least she would not have to deal with the jerk directly. Although his time as of late seemed to be occupied, and he usually left the theater as soon as practice was done. No doubt the little blond she had seen before had something to do with that.

"So," she whispered, leaning closer to Todd. "What scenes

are up for today?"

One of Spence's rules was that as soon as the actors stepped foot into the auditorium, they assumed all the qualities of their characters. It seemed strange at first, but it did help character development. Besides, it gave Lori a valid excuse to escape the world of Lorelei Sommers for a while. And that was always a welcomed change.

Todd furrowed his dark brows as he glanced at the script he held. "I think we're perfecting the wedding scene."

"Oh, great! That means the dancers and bagpipes get most of the workout. I should have stayed home."

Todd glanced around the auditorium as if looking for someone.

"What's the matter?"

"I was just checking to see if Spence was here yet." He raked his fingers through his hair as he released a quiet sigh.

Lori wanted to laugh at his worried expression. "Why are you so uptight about our Mr. Berg? You don't have to bend yourself backward to please him, you know. He's just an ordinary man."

"I don't know." Todd faced her evenly. "He may be a strict director, but that guy is really talented. This will be a first-rate performance by the time he's done with it."

Lori knew he was right but she was not in the mood for this. She was not sure how much more praise she could stand hearing from the Ice Berg's ever-faithful entourage. "Well, don't you think the actors have some influence on how the show comes off?"

"Oh, sure. But I just consider it a privilege to be working under him again. He's really gonna go places one day."

Seeing the admiration shining in Todd's dark eyes, Lori realized it was useless to argue. She shrugged and headed toward the darkness of backstage. Lately, the stillness there had given her the respite she had needed from having to deal with

Spence. . .or rather having to avoid him.

She really had no reason to complain. Spence had been nothing but professional since their little "incident." Yet that very fact bothered her the most. If he had acted cold or angry or anything except unnervingly quiet, she could have handled it. She was used to confrontation. She was not used to this.

Pushing back one of the many heavy curtain panels that dissected the backstage, Lori slipped into the familiar spot that she now thought of as hers. She froze in her tracks when she heard a hushed voice. No one was usually back here this early before rehearsal. Holding her breath, she strained to hear who it might be and what they were doing here, anyway. It was hard to tell, as the speaker was barely using a whisper.

She shifted the next panel aside and tiptoed into a larger, open area. In the faint light, she squinted and made out the form of one person who seemed to be sitting on the floor. Lori glanced around but saw no one else in sight. Whoever this was, he was talking to himself.

"Lord, I pray that today's rehearsal will go well. I ask for Your wisdom in my direction and that my actions will be glorifying to You. I know so many people here who need You. . . ."

Lori frowned as she listened. She had not had any idea that Spence ever came back here, much less to pray. So this was what Mr. Religion did prior to rehearsal. . .he was back here, petitioning his God for the salvation of the theater group. With a smirk, she turned to leave.

"And Father," Spence's utterance made her pause, "I just want to especially lift up Lori today. She's been in my heart and on mind for the last several weeks. Please give me the patience and discernment to know how to talk to her. She's a very special woman. I know that, and You know that. Help her to see it, too."

Lori stood stiff. A barrage of emotions tumbled inside as

she vacillated between storming the scene before her or running away. She remained rigid as Spence ended with a gentle, "Amen," and she watched as he stood up from his kneeling position.

Suddenly she knew exactly what Spence was doing. He knew she was here. That is why he had mentioned her like that, so she would hear it all. Likely some ploy to get her to forgive him and try and start over. No way! She would not be a fool twice.

She crossed her arms and waited for him to address her. It was just like the time in the orchestra pit when he had sensed her there. Well, she was ready this time. Biting her lower lip, she reveled in what was about to take place. Spence would beg her forgiveness, ask for another chance at friendship, all so that he might try and convert her later, she was sure of that. She would mock him, make him squirm. He would not have the upper hand this time. This time *she* would be in control.

Lori's eyes had adjusted to the dimness of the curtained-in area. She drew in a deep breath when she saw Spence turning around and she awaited his approach. Her coy smile faded as she watched him firmly gripping the curtains off to his other side. Hand over hand, he led himself away toward the stage's wings.

He had not even acknowledged her. He had known she was there. . .hadn't he? Where was he going? Shaking with confused rage, Lori whirled around and swung at the first thing that came in contact with her clenched fist. The limp curtain did little to dissipate her anger. Not caring who heard her, she stomped off toward the opposite wing.

He had done it again. How on earth could he be so exasperating when he was not even trying?

Lori's thoughts were in such a muddle as she bulldozed her way through the wings that she was not aware of anyone else around her—until she piled into poor, old Maggie.

"Whoa! Well, Lori dear. Where's the fire?" The kind, round face smiled at her.

"Sorry." Lori tried to keep her eyes toward the floor. She knew she was not crying, but this was the closest she had felt to it in years.

"Are you sure you're all right, love?" Maggie's strong hands gripped her shoulders.

Lori managed a slight nod before skittering away and down the steps to the haven of the makeup room. She hoped that that would be empty. She needed some place quiet to sort out what had just happened.

Relief washed over her when she saw the vacant room. Settling into one of the makeup booths, she flipped on the row of lights that surrounded the large mirror. Eyeing herself critically for several moments, Lori finally grimaced and flicked the switch off. She did not need to remind herself who was staring back at her.

What was the matter with her? When had she lost control of it all?

A small white pamphlet on the corner of the counter caught her eye and she reached for it. It seemed to be a brochure of some kind. The words on the front simply stated, "Come Visit Our Family." Opening it curiously, she found the address of a local church and a few candid snapshots of several people she guessed to be members. She glanced again at the name of the place: Abundant Life Fellowship. The address was not familiar.

Several voices drifted in from the hall, and she hastily placed the paper back where she had found it.

Erica breezed into the room with several members of the women's chorus. "Hi, Lori. Didn't know you were here."

"Am I needed out there yet?"

"No, they're still doing the choreography for the wedding. Easy day."

"I'll say." Lori rolled her eyes as she stood up from her chair. "Actually, I think I'll head home. It doesn't look like the leads will be in for much, right?"

Erica nodded her head. "Even my character, Jean, who's supposed to be the one getting married, is pretty quiet today."

By this time the other women had retrieved their belongings and were exiting.

"So," Erica grabbed her purse as well, "any plans for tonight?"

"No. I'm a little restless, though. Maybe I'll check into what's going on at the Regency. There must be something to do somewhere."

"The Regency? Really?" Erica's eyebrows shot up in surprise. "I thought you were sick of places like that."

"I don't know. Maybe. . .maybe not."

Her friend eyed her. "You know, I kind of thought Spence didn't like those places, either."

"Spence!" Lori's composure shattered. "Spence! Why would it matter if Spence didn't like it?"

Erica's arms flew up and down urging Lori to lower her voice. "Lori! Calm down. You don't have to blow a gasket on me. I just thought that maybe you and Spence—"

"Well, we're not!" Lori hoped her face did not look as hot as it felt.

"That's pretty obvious." Erica widened her eyes as she turned to leave.

"And that's the way I like it!" Lori called after her.

The room was empty once more, but a ringing still filled her ears. What was wrong with her emotions lately?

Angry at Erica for being so assuming and at herself for being so temperamental, Lori scooped up her duffel bag and headed for the door. At the last minute, she swung around and snatched the small pamphlet from the table.

❧

Spence eased onto the piano bench and massaged the muscles in his sore neck.

"Long day?" Mike asked.

Spence smiled. "One of the longest. I'd almost forgotten how hectic this schedule can be."

"Well," Mike sympathized, "I'm sure having a deadline to meet for those songs adds that much more pressure. How're they coming, anyway?"

"Pretty good. You wanna hear what I've got so far?"

"Sure."

Spence slid over to make room for his friend and began the intro to the first song. "This is the one with the 'country' feel to it. They want to make sure I'm diverse in my writing, I guess." He played several bars before heading into the second number.

"Don't I get to hear the words?"

Spence smiled slyly. "Not until I say 'record.' "

"Thanks a lot!" Mike's elbow nudged him gently in the ribs.

"Okay, just a hint of this one. I'll give you the chorus." Spence leaned into the emotion of the slow ballad, pressing the keys with intensity. He played through the first verse and confidently sang out when the chorus came around:

> "Can't we try just one more time?
> Take my hand and you will see
> there are oh, so many reasons
> you should belong to me.
> Please, let's try it one last time.
> Apart our souls will bleed.
> We know that in each other's arms
> together's all we need."

The last notes drifted off into the emptiness of the theater, and Spence sat, waiting for a response.

"Well, buddy. I'm impressed." A hearty slap between Spence's shoulder blades reaffirmed that fact. "There's no way they'll turn you down."

"Thanks. Actually, I'm not really done with the verses yet. I'm having a hard time with what I want to say."

"You'll do fine. They'll love 'em." Mike paused. "But isn't this a religious company? The words on that one sounded pretty . . .normal."

Spence laughed at his friend's description. "Thanks. Glad to hear they don't sound demented. But, yes, the company is Christian. One of their goals is to target listeners on other radio stations, hoping to pull them into a concert or something where they'll hear the Gospel presented by the same performer."

"Sort of a missionary type thing, huh?"

"Exactly. You know, Mike, you surprise me sometimes with the things you come out with. You seem to have a broader knowledge of spiritual things than you let on."

"Yeah," Mike cleared his throat before chuckling. "You know me. Pastor Shelton."

The two sat silent for several seconds. "Any new developments with Lori?"

Spence shook his head. "Nope." That was all he really cared to share. As far as he knew, Lori had not told anyone about their last encounter, and he would rather it stayed that way as well.

"Well, I'd better run." Mike stood and patted Spence's shoulder once more. "See you tomorrow, bright and early."

Spence waved him off before collecting his satchel of music and his tape recorder. He had to get home himself and try to work on that song. There had to be some way to get those verses to come to him.

❧

Pushing open the door to his apartment, Spence heard the phone jangling. He dropped his bag on the floor and hurried to answer it.

"Hello?"

"Hello, Spencer?" the woman's voice came across the wire.

"Yes?"

"This is Dr. Greene."

"Oh, hello there." Spence's mind then recalled the young opthalmologist who had taken a special interest in his eye treatments after the accident. "What's up? Did I miss an appointment?" He tried to remember if he was supposed to have had one recently.

"No, no," she laughed. "I'm calling with some other news. I have something I thought you might be interested in."

"Really? What's that, new eyes?" He smiled at his comment.

"Well, in a sense, we might."

She sounded quite serious, and Spence cleared his throat a few times before responding. "What do you mean, exactly?"

"There's a doctor here who specializes in corneal transplant surgery. He would like to have a look at your eyes and run a few tests to determine the extent of your scarring."

"You can't be serious. I thought my eyes were beyond help. That the scars were too deep." Spence felt his breath quicken. He could not get too hopeful from a simple phone call. After all, they had already declared him blind without any hope for improvement.

"Now this is purely for testing purposes. There aren't any guarantees or promises. He simply wants to see you for himself."

Well, that sounded more realistic. Spence felt his breathing return to normal while his heart sank several inches.

"Sure, I guess that would be okay. Um, I'm pretty busy now with my rehearsals and things."

"Is there any time available within the next week or two?"

"Yeah, I guess I could skip out one afternoon."

"Wonderful. What day would be best for you?"

"Um," Spence pondered as he kneaded his forehead. "I guess next Wednesday would work out the easiest for me. My sister will be able to come with me then."

"That sounds great. I'll set up an appointment with Dr. Bray."

Spence listened carefully to all her instructions about where the examination would take place. Confident he could remember the information, he thanked the doctor and hung up the phone.

He did not want to get himself worked up into a false state of hopefulness, but he could not smother the giddiness he felt pushing up in his chest. At least the opportunity had arisen to find out if there was a chance. Even that was something for which to be thankful.

No longer trying to control the sappy grin on his face, Spence clutched the phone once more and dialed.

"Hello, Berg residence," a familiar voice sounded.

"Hi, Mom. Guess what?"

seven

Lori glanced first at her watch, then at the gas gauge. How long could she just drive around? She had explored all the neighborhoods she knew and several that were not familiar to her. The endless driving was getting tiresome. There had to be something to do besides going home.

The next red stoplight gave her a chance to note her location. Fifth Street. Say, wasn't that near. . .? She pulled a hard right into the turning lane and drove onto the bisecting street. Parking at the curb, she scrounged around in her duffel bag until the small white pamphlet showed itself. Looking at the front cover warily, she memorized the address and pulled back out into the traffic, wondering if it would be difficult to find.

It wasn't. Five minutes and several blocks later found her staring at 7819 Fifth Street. The façade surprised Lori. She had been expecting a large cathedral complete with the ever-present looming spires receding into the clouds. Parallel parking her Corvette, she switched off the ignition and continued her study of the building from across the street.

Hanging from one of the two large windows that enclosed the front of what looked to be a vacant store or warehouse, a neat, yet nonflashy sign announced the facility of Abundant Life Fellowship. This was a church?

She smirked at its deceptive appearance. At least they tried to blend into the woodwork while they suckered people through their doors. Someone a little less knowledgeable might even risk entering, thinking it would be different than all the other gothic-looking antiquities that graced the Twin Cities. At least she knew better. They were all basically the same: Jesus loves you, join our flock, give us money.

Calling herself every stupid name she could think of, Lori fingered the ignition key. There was no point in sticking around. Truthfully, she wondered why she had even come. *That's what I get for acting on my weak emotions.* Just about to start the engine, she hesitated. Her eyes caught another large sign taped to the inside of the window: I CAME THAT YOU MIGHT HAVE LIFE AND HAVE IT MORE ABUNDANTLY.

At least she knew where their name came from now. . .some Scripture verse. Life abundantly. . .she tried to reason out what that might mean. Only rich people had abundant life, didn't they? Immediate thoughts of her father contradicted that notion. Her parents had plenty of money and she definitely did not want their lifestyle. *That's one of the reasons you decided to move away,* she reminded herself.

Squinting again at the foreign building, Lori weighed her options. Maybe it would not hurt just to take a peek around the place. After all, she had already driven here. She eased out of her car and glanced both ways before crossing the moderately busy street.

The glass double doors seemed to stare at her in challenge. Reaching out a shaking hand, she curled her fingers around the handle. Just as she was about to pull it open, she saw a barrage of people swarm toward the front from a partitioned area in the rear. Lori dropped her grip and scrambled down the sidewalk, ducking into a narrow alley along the side of the building.

She waited several seconds before peering around the brick wall. A small group of young people about her age stood chatting and laughing. Her breath caught in her throat when she recognized Spence's familiar wiry frame. His back was to her and his hands were pushed deep into the pockets of his jeans as he rocked with laughter.

Rising up on her tiptoes, Lori tried to see the person making him laugh as she had never seen him laugh before. Just then,

Spence sidestepped and the woman standing before him came into view. Lori frowned. The woman looked vaguely familiar. Studying her shoulder-length brown hair and her incredibly tiny frame, Lori finally recalled her as one of the new people who had shown up for the auditions. She also remembered snickering along with Erica over the woman's obvious lack of experience. To say that she had not considered the small woman a threat would be an understatement. That is. . .not until now.

Curling her fingers into her palms, Lori watched in disturbed fascination as the bubbly little thing produced peals of laughter from the usually all-business Spence.

Thoroughly embarrassed and humiliated, Lori knew it was time to leave. She could not just stand there and continue to watch. Not caring who saw her, she stepped deliberately onto the sidewalk and prepared to cross the street as quickly as possible. She had nowhere to go but home. . .so what. One more time, she told herself that in the end there was no one to depend on but Lori. It had always been that way, and it would never change.

Once inside the safety of her car, Lori let out a long breath. She ignored the desire to cast one last glance in Spence's direction as she slammed the car into gear and swerved out into the street.

"Hey," Diane said suddenly, touching Spence's sleeve. "I think that was Lori Sommers."

"Really?" Spence automatically spun around to try and find her. Some habits died hard. He turned back toward Diane. "Is she still here?"

"No, she just crossed the street, got into her car, and then drove off. Does she go to church here, too?"

"Uh, no," Spence answered. "I don't think she goes to church."

"Really?" Diane's small voice registered concern. "I'll be sure to remember her in my prayers then."

"You do that, Diane. She could use as many prayers as the

two of us can send up." He paused. "Well, if you'll excuse me, I should catch the next bus home. It's getting late."

"All right. We'll see you at rehearsal tomorrow." Diane hesitated for a moment. "And thanks for sharing your exciting news at church tonight. I'll be praying about that, too."

Spence smiled at her thoughtfulness. "I appreciate it. Right now, even the possibility of regaining my sight seems a little too good to be true."

"As Pastor Schell says, 'Trust God to do His Will.' "

"Thanks. I'll hold that thought." He reached out and squeezed her shoulder before turning to head toward the bench at the bus stop.

The Q line stopped right on schedule, and Spence bounded up the steps.

"Howdy, Spencer," said the gruff-voiced driver who had become his friend since riding the transit system.

"Hey, Bob."

"How was church tonight?"

Spence took one of the side-facing seats in the front and clutched the nearest rail to steady himself against the jolt of acceleration. "Just fine. Had a few new things to pray over."

"Oh, yeah?" Bob sounded interested.

"Yep. Goin' to see the doctor next week about a possible surgery for my eyes."

"Yer kiddin'!"

"Nope. Pretty exciting, huh?" Spence waited for his answer momentarily as the bus stopped again and several riders got in, depositing their coins in the meter in passing.

"I'll say," the older man continued. "God's doin' some mighty things in your life."

Spence felt his mouth curving into a lopsided grin. It seemed Bob always had a lesson to teach Spence about the awesomeness of the Lord and his own humility. Little did he know of this a year ago when he had first starting conversing with his new friend after church.

Showing great interest in the new little denomination, Bob had constantly drilled Spence with questions about it, its beliefs, and about Scripture. . .an endless barrage of inquiries. One conversation would always stand out in Spence's memory. He could recall it verbatim, and it still warmed his heart whenever it came to mind.

"So," Bob had clarified. "God sent His Son to die for the whole world. Even for Bob Felland, a regular old bus driver."

"You're not so regular, Bob," Spence had insisted. "God loves you as the very special and unique person He made you to be. Besides, being a regular old bus driver is quite a service. A lot of people depend on you. That's pretty important, don't you think?"

"I never thought of it that way." His growling voice had stopped for a moment as if to do just that. "But you know what, Spencer?"

"What?" Spence had prepared himself for an argument on the validity of the Bible.

"None of this matters."

"What do you mean? I just told you how many, many people depend on—"

"No, no. I mean this job I do doesn't matter unless I'm doing something like you're doin'—talkin' to me here. Furthering His kingdom, isn't that what you called it?"

"Yeah," Spence had said almost to himself. "Showing others the way."

"Well," Bob had pointed out. "What good would it do if there were no maps for people to study on which bus goes where? And it would mess things up a whole lot if I didn't display my route letter on the front of my bus, wouldn't it?"

Spence had grinned as he saw where the driver's comparison was headed. Things had not been put this plainly to him since he had heard a children's sermon as a boy. Maybe that is what everyone needed from time to time—clear, unadulterated word-pictures on the love of God and His plan of salvation.

"So, the way I see it, God has given us that there Bible as a map and Jesus is sort of the navigator, the right bus we're supposed to catch. God clearly marked Him as the only way to get to heaven."

Spence had swallowed hard, keenly aware of the tears in his eyes. Nothing this rewarding had ever happened to him. He had leaned forward and placed a hand on the rough work shirt that covered Bob's broad shoulders. "Welcome home, buddy."

"Thanks," he had said, the grin quite apparent in his voice. "You done good at tellin' me everything."

"Bob," Spence had laughed. "If this is witnessing, I think Christians are making things more complicated than they need be. I wonder who taught whom more in these exchanges."

Bob's coarse chuckle had answered. "We learn from each other."

Still sighing deeply over the remembered conversation, Spence answered Bob's latest question. "Yeah, I guess God certainly does move in some strange and mysterious ways."

"Well," Bob said as the bus's brakes squealed it to a stop. "Here's home. I'll be prayin' for ya on that possible surgery."

"You and a lot of others, Bob. Thanks. I appreciate it." Spence felt the bus driver's large hand give him a friendly slap on the back as he deftly descended the few steps to the sidewalk and got his bearings with his cane. Giving one last wave to the receding roar of the bus, he strode toward his apartment building.

Once inside, he flopped down on his plump, comfortable couch. Tiredness pervaded his whole being, but the excitement he felt at the same time continued to course through his veins.

Letting out a long breath, Spence headed for his bedroom and stopped at the window above his headboard. Pushing upward on the sticky sash, the sounds of the city poured into his room. Cars whizzed by on the street below. Off in the distance the wail of a siren echoed, and from the center of the old downtown, the cry of a train whistle lingered in the still air.

He knew the cleanliness of Minneapolis air far exceeded most other metropolitan areas. Visions of the large number of trees and lakes right inside the city proper still came easily to his memory. A year of being without sight had not taken away his appreciation for the beauty of his surroundings. But he knew he also missed the north. The country where the stars were so densely clustered in the evening sky that sometimes it appeared more white than black.

Shutting his window with a sigh of resignation, Spence slowly dressed for bedand crawled between the coolness of his sheets. Soon enough, after the musical was done, he would be able to venture north again.

His heart fluttered for a moment before he squashed its premature longings that perhaps the next time he would head upstate he might be able to see the never-ending rows of pines, standing like sentinels along the roads, or to watch the glorious soaring of the hawk above the glass surface of a reflective lake.

He knew he had dealt with his injury fairly well, but he did, especially in this season of the year, miss the majesty of God's creation. And whatever happened, he would always treasure his myriad of mental pictures.

God, he prayed, *You know what will come of this appointment next week. I just ask that You give me patience and understanding of Your leading.* He paused for a moment and remembered Diane's comment about seeing Lori earlier. He lifted his petition again. *And Lord, I pray for Lori. If she was near church this evening, I pray that someway, somehow she'll find the encouragement and desire to visit. . . .*

Feeling suddenly convicted, Spence halted his prayer.

Encouragement? A stinging realization hit him full force. He had done nothing lately to foster any attempts at building a bridge toward her. He had been nothing but. . .formal. *Is that how you want her to see Christians?*

❧

Lori put her car keys in the attendant's hand, dropped the claim ticket in her handbag, and ran a hand over her black silk chemise to smooth out any wrinkles. She continued up the carpeted walkway from the carport, noting the small number of people there. . .even for a Wednesday. There was usually something big going on at the Regency.

She had to take one more quick breath of fortitude as she faced the sparkling entrance. How long had it been since she had been to a place like this? Over a year? Not since she had moved to Minneapolis.

Back in Florida, the Hilton had been the hotel of choice for all the political hullabaloo surrounding her father. She remembered how elegant it had seemed when she was a little girl. How she would pretend she was a princess, traipsing about her castle. Even as a teen-ager, when the greed and back stabbing of the state's political races no longer escaped her, she found the long, empty corridors and the decorous rooms a needed diversion from the onslaught of attention she received for being the daughter of the lieutenant governor.

Giving herself a mental shake, Lori pulled back her shoulders and marched toward the door. She could do this. She *would* do this. Over a year of being sequestered was far too long. This was a different place, a different city. No one would ever know. It could be like it had been when she was a child.

A smiling doorman gave a curt nod as he pulled open the door for her.

Once inside the subtly lit foyer, Lori paused on the plush crimson rug and debated about which direction to head. The lobby's scheduling board was pretty scant of activities, although she did not stop to read them closely.

Out of habit, she started toward the cocktail lounge. Through the round, glass double doors, she was met by the plunking of a soft jazz piano and the rich, brilliant glow from around the sunken brass bar.

Once at the railing, she was greeted by the friendly bartender. "Good evening, miss. What may I get for you?"

Lori was about to order her usual beverage when a burst of laughter from a group across the room interrupted her. The small gathering consisted of about ten men in very fine, three-piece suits. They could have been any professionals. She started to turn her attention back to the smiling man before her when one of the distant faces caught her eye. The sandy-haired man looked painfully familiar. She took a quick breath and studied him carefully.

"Made up your mind yet?"

"What?" She swung her gaze back in front of her for a brief moment. "Uh, yes. Well. . .I'll have. . . ." She looked again at the man on the other side of the room. In low tones, he was relating something to the other fellows. "Tell me. . .who exactly are those guys over there? Do you know?" Lori nodded in their direction.

"Them? I think they're a bunch of politicians, to tell you the truth. Up here for some convention."

A large lump rose quickly in her throat.

"Now, can I get you something?"

She nodded. "Club soda." Then she prayed he would hurry as she discreetly turned her back to the conversing men.

Once her glass was in hand, she paid for her drink and then rose abruptly from her stool. "Think I'll enjoy this out by the pool." The bartender nodded and continued wiping down the already spotless counter.

Lori slipped out a side door and found herself in the center atrium and pool area. Now that the darkness of night had fallen, the small lamps placed along the stone path cast a romantic, surreal glow on the bushes and trees. She followed the winding sidewalk toward the sound of the splashing water. A fountain in the middle of the pool shot up nearly twenty feet as underwater lights colored the spray in various pastels.

Lori scarcely noticed the beauty of the place. Her mind kept shooting back to the young man's face in the lounge. An involuntary shiver skittered down her spine and she felt the skin on her arms prickle. *It couldn't have been him,* she reassured herself. *It's been over a year.* With the exception of her father's monthly phone calls, there had been no contact from them. There'd been no reason for any.

You're paranoid, Lori, she chided herself. She stepped over to the small footbridge that arched across the pool and leaned on the rail. *You came here to have a nice, quiet evening, remember?* She managed a nervous laugh.

"Pretty sad when a beautiful woman has only herself to talk to."

Lori's fingers fumbled and her glass dropped into the sparkling water below. She sought vainly for the source of the low voice but saw no one. With her heart nearly pounding out of her chest, she began gingerly backing off the bridge.

A rustle in the bushes directly behind her caused her to wheel around in terror. Still, no one. She eyed the path heading back to the lounge. Would it be safe?

"Let's just hope," a voice warned from behind Lori, "that the bright young lady doesn't forget who she can. . .and *can't* talk to." He broke off ominously.

Unable to endure any more, she ran blindly through the remainder of the twisting path, oblivious to the errant branches and twigs that raked across her face and arms.

She finally reached the lounge door and, with gasping breaths, yanked on the doorknob. A panicked cry escaped her lips. The door did not budge. It couldn't be locked, it just couldn't! The shimmy of the leaves in a nearby cluster of trees gave her a surge of adrenaline. She twisted and yanked on the stubborn handle until her arms ached.

At last, the sticky latch worked free, and she flung herself into the room. Not even taking time to notice if there was anyone else in the lounge, she sprinted out into the hall and headed for the lobby. With a curious look, the front desk clerk glanced up from his work.

She tried to slow her pace as she approached him, digging through her handbag at the same time. "C36," she stated breathlessly as she threw the claim ticket on the counter before him. "The red Corvette."

He nodded, studying her cautiously, and picked up the phone.

A cluster of people entered the lobby, talking and laughing as they approached the front doors. Lori turned toward the desk, head down. It was then that she noticed the myriad of scratches on her arm. No wonder the clerk had regarded her so strangely. She must look a fright. She tried to run her fingers through her tangled hair.

"Your car will be here shortly, ma'am."

She nodded a thank you and turned to head toward the front door. Her short walk was interrupted when she collided with the chest of a man wearing a black, pin-striped suit. Her heart in her throat, she slowly lifted her gaze to meet with steely blue eyes and sandy hair. She was starting to shake, and her feet seemed rooted to the spot.

A wan smile formed on his lips as he grasped her shoulders. "I'm truly sorry, ma'am. Forgive my clumsiness. Although I must say it's not often that I have the opportunity to bump into such a beautiful woman. Perhaps it won't be the last." He dropped his hands and stepped to the side.

Lori skittered around him, thankful to see her car was ready and waiting at the entrance. She grabbed the keys from the young attendant, nearly forgetting to leave a tip. She distractedly dug in her purse for a bill, pressed it into his hand, and slid into the front seat, trying not to squeal the tires in her haste to get away.

eight

With his interrupted prayer still pervading his every thought, Spence rolled over restlessly and continued to listen to the muffled noises outside his window. What was Lori doing tonight, anyway? He reached out a hand for his nightstand and fumbled with his alarm clock. "The time is 9:58 P.M."

His fingers found their way to the phone and the slow buzzing of the dial tone reached his ears as he removed the receiver from its cradle. Maybe it was too late to call. *Call.*

Pushing the digits for information, he waited until an operator picked up the line. "What city, please."

"Minneapolis."

"Yes?"

"I'd like the number for a Lorelei Sommers."

"Thank you." A moment of silence. "I have an L. Sommers at Trifalger Way."

"Yes, that's the one."

"One moment please."

The recorded message clicked on. "The number is 555-6487."

Spence pushed down the button once to disconnect the line. His fingers began to shake as he dialed the new number. A strong desire to hang up and forget about the whole notion blazed through his head. About to act on that very thought, the ringing was interrupted by the click of an answering machine.

He breathed a sigh of relief. At least he would not have to talk to her directly. . .yet.

"Hello," her well-modulated voice answered. "You've reached the home of the world famous actress. . .the next Ethel Barrymore. . .the next. . . ." Lori's light laughter followed for a moment. "Lori Sommers. Can't come to the phone just now, but I hate to miss your call. Please leave your message after the beep." Two short blips followed and then a long tone.

Spence cleared his throat, hoping his voice would not betray the warmth he felt on his face. "Uh, hello, Lori? This is Spence. I was, um, just calling to say hi and to. . .see how you're doing. I guess I'll see you tomorrow at rehearsal. Bye for now."

He gently hung up and rolled over onto his back. For some reason he just did not feel right. Shutting his eyes tightly, he continued his previous prayer.

"Okay, God. You can see her. Reach out and hold her wherever she is. . .whatever she's doing."

❧

Lori wrapped her heavy chenille robe more tightly around her knees as she scooted into the corner of her sectional sofa. The buzzing of the answering machine finally stopped, and a series of clicks set it back into answering mode.

"Spence," she whispered, swallowing the growing lump in her throat.

She continued to stare out the expansive window overlooking a well-lit section of the city, where the towering office building windows competed with traffic lights and the red blur of taillights. Grabbing the comb from beside her, she began to pull it through her damp tangles, ignoring the painful jabs in her scalp as she ripped through the snarls.

How long would she stay like this, anyway? Sitting locked in her apartment, waiting. It was no way to spend her evening . . .her life.

Not even thirty seconds had passed when the telephone rang again. Lori's heart lurched within her. Was it Spence again? She stopped pulling the comb through her hair, staring hopelessly at the end table where the clear acrylic phone taunted her.

Her fingers ached to pick it up. . .to see if it was indeed Spence. If it was anybody besides. . . .

"Hello," her answering machine answered once again. Lori waited for the message to run its course.

"Lori," a deep, angry voice resounded for the hundredth time that evening. "This is your father! Pick up the phone. Now!"

Chills quivered up and down her spine. "Not on your life," she said in a low voice. She could endure hours of harassment via the phone. At least he was not here. And again she was relieved at the several-hundred-mile distance separating them.

"I know you're there," her father continued. Another long pause. "Okay, princess, play your games. We know where you were tonight. Just let me give you a little something to think on. Think of life without a car. . .without your pretty little condo. Maybe even living back here in Florida."

He stopped momentarily, as if giving her time to let it all sink in. "How would you like that, Lori, hmm? Living back here. . .with Daddy."

She heard the click of the line and, in a fraction of a second, she vaulted from the couch and yanked the telephone cord straight out of the jack.

Living back here with Daddy?

The name struck such anger and fury in her heart, she whirled around and knocked a delicate, framed watercolor from the wall. Daddy, indeed. How many *daddies* paid off on rent for their little girls? Unbidden, the memories came crashing in around her. . .the ones that refused to go away.

"You're fifteen now, Lori. Old enough to start making your appearances with your mother and me. The lieutenant governor's family is expected to be in the public eye. Get used to it."

The dogged schedule, the hordes of reporters, the talk of Governor Carlyle running for the presidency, her father. . .a cabinet officer.

Streamers, balloons, banners covering every inch of the Hilton Hotel's largest ballroom. CARLYLE. . .JACOBS—ALL THE WAY!

"Smile pretty, Lori. These shots will be in all the papers tomorrow."

"I'm tired, Mom. I want to go back to my room."

Her mother and father in deep conversation with some important businessmen. Campaign contributions.

"Mom, I'm really tired."

"All right, dear." A distracted pat on the shoulder. "Go on up. We'll stop by your room on the way down to breakfast."

Aching feet carrying her to her sanctuary from the madness. Pushing through the door and closing it in relief behind her.

Suddenly, a strong grip on her forearm. A cry of panic. A sidelight flicked on to reveal Governor Carlyle's son, John.

The predatory look in his eyes. The rough, whiskered nearness. The reek of strong alcohol and the thick breath. Then no face, no mental pictures. Watery eyes shut tightly against the thief of her innocence, the marauder of her youth. There was no turning back now. . .she had "grown up" whether she had wanted to or not.

Endless dinner parties with the Carlyle family. Hearty laughter echoing around the farce of the intimate gathering. She could not eat. . .bile rose upward in her throat, choking out the words she could not bear to utter anyway.

"You're such a pretty girl, Lori." The blurry face of a round Mrs. Carlyle from across the table. "You must have boys just following you all over the place. Perhaps you and John could get better acquainted."

Twittered laughter. A weak half-smile forced upon Lori's lips. If this woman only knew.

The house now empty of guests. "Next time, you'll be more polite. Do you understand me?" Donald Jacob's large hand cinched tightly around her arm, his icy blue eyes staring holes into her. An unspoken—and even more sinister—command. "I don't know where you came up with this ridiculous story, but true or not, it's not going to ruin the lives of everyone in this household. There's an election going on here, little miss. It's trouble enough that Ted Carlyle was willing to reimburse us for the little incident. But I'll hear no more about it. Understood?"

A quick nervous nod.

One last warning look before studying her flushed face. "You probably asked for it, anyway."

Lori's body shuddered at the nightmare. Only it was no nightmare—this was her life. She scanned the area around her, taking in all the things that were *hers* in return for their deal. Nice things. Lovely things. And the mere sight of them made her sick.

Turning back around, she snatched up the couch cushions and flung them about the room. Systematically, she hurled every last article that came from *them* out of her path. Oh, how she hated him. Daddy, what a joke. Donald Jacobs was no father to her. She was Lori *Sommers* now. She had seen to that as soon as she had turned eighteen. She wanted no part of his name or him. Yet here she was, still playing his games. And long ago he had broken all the rules.

Letting out a cry of anguish, Lori crumpled to a heap on the floor, trembling, gasping for breath after her tirade. She knew this had to stop. But she did not know when. . .or how.

❧

"Okay, guys, that was great!" Spence called out to the actors on stage. "Todd, just make sure that you're by the spot at the tree to fit the timing of the song. Otherwise, you and Lori are doing a fantastic job."

"Thanks, Spence." Todd's voice registered pleasure in itself.

No comment came from Lori.

"Well," Spence sat back down at the piano. "I appreciate you two staying late to work on the 'Heather on the Hill' scene. If you're both comfortable with it, I guess that's it. You can head home."

"Okay." The creaking wooden stage steps protested at Todd's exit. "See you tomorrow, Spence."

"Yep." Spence waved a goodbye.

He began sorting through the miscellaneous papers and audio tapes cluttering the top of the baby grand. Knowing it was only about nine o'clock, he decided to run through his songs one more time. There were only two days before he would step into the recording studio to make his demo tape. The Way Music Corporation wanted it by the end of June, and so far the time line seemed to be working out.

"All righty," Spence muttered to himself, "let's see if we can perfect these babies a little bit."

He stretched his arms over his head and tilted his head from side to side, loosening the tense muscles in his neck.

Opting to start with the country song, he coaxed the slow, rhythmic beginning out of his fingers, then broke into the melody:

> "She slipped her tiny fingers
> into her daddy's great big hand,
> studying the callouses
> he'd earned from working land."

Spence stopped, suddenly feeling uncomfortable. Taking a deep breath and releasing it, he realized why. "Lori?" his voice ventured in the expanse of the empty theater.

"Yes," she answered meekly after a slight pause.

Spence chuckled with some relief. "Well, Miss Sommers. Do you know you gave me a small scare there? I wasn't sure if

I was all alone in this place with a crazed lunatic or what."

"No," she replied softly. "Only half-crazed."

"Oh, well good. That makes two of us."

Spence wondered what to say next. It had been weeks since they had spoken to one another. Should he mention the telephone call he had made the night before? Had she even received the message?

"Thanks for calling me last night."

Spence smirked as he dropped his head toward the piano keys. "Sure."

"I, um," Lori hedged, "I was having kind of a bad night. Otherwise I would have called you back."

Spence raised his head once again and began gathering his belongings together. "Would you have really?" He did not want to accuse her of being a liar, but he also wanted to start over with a clean slate between them, one with no half-truths or assumptions.

"Yes," her voice was stronger now. "I would have. Really."

"Good."

Several minutes of uncomfortable silence followed.

Spence wished there was some graceful way he could excuse himself. Then he inwardly kicked himself because this could be what he had been praying would happen for weeks—another chance to start their friendship anew.

"Are those your new songs? The ones for your contract?" Lori sounded interested, but she made no effort to come any closer, staying in her place on the stage.

"Yeah, that was one of them."

"I liked the beginning. I'd like to hear more."

Spence's mind flashed for a moment, and he spoke with new boldness. "I'm, uh, going to the studio on Saturday to cut the songs. Would you like to come along?" This might be an excellent, yet unobtrusive way to witness to her. "Mike will be coming, too," he added, wanting to clarify that it would not constitute a date. After their last dinner, he hardly worried that she would be interested in one, anyhow.

"Okay," she agreed. "I'd like that."

"Good."

Another silence. Was this going to take longer than he thought? They had talked so freely before. . .oh yeah, before. Had he ever blown it. He began to seriously doubt what kind of witness he could provide after nearly losing it that night. Coming so close to compromising his beliefs would not help the cause any, especially with someone as far out on the fringes as Lori seemed to be. She needed to know that Christians not only talked differently, but lived differently as well.

"Are you busy tonight?" Her question broke the heavy silence.

Oh, boy, here they went again. "Well," Spence stalled.

"If you are, it's okay," she interrupted.

"It's kind of late. I'm not sure anything would be open by the time. . . ." He tapered off in hesitation. Something told him that she needed company this evening. "Well, Lake of the Isles doesn't ever close. We could walk around that if you'd like."

"Oh, that would be fine." She sounded quite relieved.

"Okay, let's head out. We're well within walking distance. I'll, um, leave my stuff here for now, I guess. I can get it later." Spence turned and stepped up the slight staircase that brought him out of the orchestra pit. Lori was instantly at his side, but she made no move to link her arm through his as she had done before. He sensed an uneasiness in her, and he hoped it was not because of him.

Lori followed Spence out the theater door and reached out to clasp his hand, placing it firmly near her elbow. She tried to ignore the rush of warmth it sent up her arm. "You ready?"

"All set," he replied grinning. "Do you know where you're going?"

"No," Lori laughed as they started off. "I was hoping you would be navigator."

"Boy, lady, you certainly know how to pick 'em. A blind navigator. . . ." He tossed a teasing smile her way.

They walked in silence for several minutes. Lori was not sure if that was a good sign or not. Maybe this had not been such a good idea.

She glanced over at Spence, who seemed to be quite content. An easy smile played with his one dimple and, once again, Lori found herself fascinated by the character of his face. He seemed to get infinitely more handsome each time she saw him.

The intermittent breeze ruffled that endearing cowlick of his, blowing it across his forehead. She longed to brush it away . . .the way she had that night—

"So," Lori interrupted her own thoughts, "are you pleased with how the musical is coming?"

"Sure am," he said, nodding. "You and Todd are doing a bang-up job. As usual."

Lori flushed slightly, realizing it sounded like she had been fishing for a compliment. She wished that she would learn a few social graces to get her through discomforting situations like this. But, she reminded herself, this was her idea. She lapsed into another round of quietness.

The sounds of the city at night filled in where their conversation faltered. The headlights of an occasional, passing car lit up the sidewalk before them while the sounds of the traffic on the main thoroughfare provided a steady hum.

Doors and windows were opened on nearby houses, graciously inviting in the coolness of the early summer evening. Lori studied some of the immense homes along the tree-lined street. Many displayed large turrets and long, wide porches strewn with lush plants, and all contained countless windows from which the occupants could meditate on the serene area along the lake.

"Minneapolis really is a beautiful city, you know?" Lori stated thoughtfully.

"As far as cities go, I agree."

"Don't you like the city?" She returned her gaze to Spence.

"Oh, it's okay. Like you said, Minneapolis, and St. Paul, too, are probably some of the prettiest. But my heart always yearns for the north."

"The north," Lori chuckled. "Being from Florida, Minneapolis is about as far north as I can imagine."

"I suppose." Spence smiled. "Tell me about Florida. What's it like, anyway?"

"It's hot. It's humid. It's crowded."

"Wow." Spence's eyebrows shot up from behind his dark glasses. "Sounds great," he added sarcastically.

"Well," Lori informed him with a smile, "we have our pretty places, too. The Everglades are always nice to visit. They're so green and alive. . . ." She let the thought dangle. She was not used to talking like this to anyone.

"Don't stop," he urged her. "It sounds interesting."

"I. . .I don't know," she stuttered. "I think this is the place." Coming to the small, placid lake lined by meandering sidewalks and wrought-iron benches, she came to a stop, glad that they had finally arrived.

Spence lifted his nose slightly and sniffed. "Fresh water, a little bit fishy. . .yeah, I'd say so." He sat down on the dewy bank. "I thought you didn't know how to get here." He lifted his face in question.

"Well," she admitted as she joined him on the grass, "I have been here a couple times."

"Oh, really? With whom?"

Lori cast him a skeptical glance. "By myself, actually. It seems to be one of those places where you can be alone."

"Do you wish you were alone now?"

"No."

"Well then," Spence plucked up several strands of grass and twirled them in his fingers, "I'm glad I'm the one to be here with you."

Lori looked over at him in awe. How could he be so nice after what she had done to him. . .how she had treated him? "You're awfully charming, you know."

He gently threw down the handful of blades. "I don't mean to be." He paused for an uncomfortable second. "I like you, Lori. I'd like to be your friend."

Lori swallowed hard and squinted her eyes as she peered across the moonlit water. How was she supposed to answer that?

"Come on." She jumped to her feet and tapped him lightly on the shoulder, letting her hand linger there. "Let's go wading."

"You're on." Spence grasped her arm and scrambled to his feet to join her. "Just don't let me lose my shoes after I take them off. These babies cost me a pretty penny."

Reaching the rocks lining the lake's shore, they plunked down on the lawn and began removing their shoes and socks. In between adolescent spurts of laughter, they admonished each other to be quiet lest they wake the neighborhood.

Lori stood and helped Spence to his feet then, biting her lip for a moment of indecision, she reached up and removed his glasses. "Why don't you leave these here? You don't want them to fall in the water." He waited patiently while she placed them with their pile of footwear. When she stood back up, she stared into his blinking, dark eyes. "Does that bother you? Do you want them back?"

"No, it's all right." He nodded slightly. "If it doesn't bother you."

Lori crossed her arms in front of her and shifted her weight to the opposite foot. "Now why would it bother me?"

Spence shrugged. "I don't know. I just thought that maybe they looked sort of—"

"Your eyes look fine," she broke in. "Besides, they're a whole lot better than those reclusive sunglasses."

He smiled at her broadly, and she found herself grinning back. "Come on!" Hauling him by the arm, they gingerly stepped down the algae-covered stones as the chilly water licked gently at their toes. Spence let out a low whistle as they ventured farther into the dark stillness.

"Kinda chilly, eh?" Lori asked through shallow breaths as the temperature finally hit her as well.

"No, it's fine," he answered in a high falsetto.

"If it's too much for you. . . ," she said in a teasing singsong.

Spence raised one eyebrow as he sent her a lopsided grin. "Don't you taunt me, Miss Sommers."

"Well," she replied in a condescending tone, "you know what they say, 'If you can't stand the heat—' "

"Try the cold," Spence interjected as he let go of her elbow and gave her a gentle yet firm push forward. A loud gasp preceded a tremendous splash and he laughed heartily.

"Sorry, Lori. That was just too tempting. I haven't done that since I was a kid with my little sister." He let out a deep sigh. Suddenly, it seemed awfully quiet.

"Lori?" He waved his arms on all sides, trying to see if she was standing anywhere within reach. Nothing.

"Lori?" The fear was starting to creep into his voice. "Lori? Are you—"

Two hands lit upon his shoulders from behind and gave a mighty push. Spence felt himself falling forward. Instinctively stretching his arms out to catch himself, the icy lake rushed around him in stunning greeting. He quickly regained his footing and stood up, his shirt clinging to his thoroughly soaked body.

"Gotcha," came her quiet, mischievous voice.

Spence shook the last droplets of water from his hair and held out his hand. "Truce? You give as good as you get, I see."

Her small hand grasped his. "Consider the white flag out."

He was not sure how long they stood like that. . .waist deep in the nipping water, the tips of their fingers brushing together. Closing his eyes, he tried to imagine the vision she must be, standing there before him.

For the first time since he had known her, Lori seemed open . . .vulnerable, reachable. For a tender moment he drank in with his touch what his eyes could not.

A chorus of crickets and frogs drew his thoughts back, and he shivered. He dropped Lori's hand. "We'll catch our death out here. Let's go."

Lori reached for his arm once more and led him silently out of the water. Neither spoke as they tugged on their socks and shoes.

Spence pushed the button on his watch but there came no response. He pushed it again and then groaned as he realized why.

"What's the matter?" Lori asked.

"I forgot to take my watch off."

"Oh. Well, let's see." She paused for a moment. "It's a little after eleven." He heard her tap the face of her timepiece.

He chuckled and gave her a playful nudge with his shoulder. "Well, smartie, we'd better get you home. What will everyone say if they know I was keeping out the star actress until odd hours of the evening?"

"Indeed, what *will* they say?" Lori's tone bristled at his comment.

Spence ran a hand through his wet hair as he sighed. "Come on, Lori. I'm just kidding. Let them think what they want."

"Really?" She sounded skeptical. "It doesn't matter to you that you might be seen with me?"

He stepped forward and pretended to remove a cap as he

bowed. "My lady, it would do me honor."

She made no further comment but stepped to his side and placed his hand in its now-familiar place on her arm. The walk back was nearly as silent as the trek to Lake of the Isles, but this time, despite the chilliness of the evening air on their damp bodies, the quiet seemed to warm him, comfort him.

The traffic increased as they approached Penny Lane, reminding Spence that a city never sleeps. The longing for the peaceful northern country tugged at his heart again. Would Lori like it as well?

After they had covered a number of blocks, Spence found himself regretting the end of this evening. It certainly had not been what he had expected. Of course, with Lori, things never were, and that was one of the things he enjoyed about her.

They would be at the doors of theater shortly. He should say something else before the night was over. "What are you thinking?" he asked softly.

"I hate wet jeans."

He laughed. Progress in their friendship would be slow, but it was definitely there. He did not try to hide the smile creeping across his face.

nine

Radiant sunshine streaked in through Lori's bedroom window, bathing her in its warmth, bringing the satin stripes of the rose wallpaper to life. With a half-awake smile, she stretched her arms over her head as she twisted her body in the smoothness of the floral sheets. She could sleep this whole morning away—provided that the dream she had been enjoying would continue. Even now she dreaded opening her eyes, afraid to lose the vision of Spence's caring, honest face that lingered tantalizingly beneath the surface of her consciousness.

The ringing of the telephone brought the inevitable, and her eyes fluttered open, squinting against the sudden brightness. Focusing her gaze on the clock, she noticed it was only 7:30. Who would be calling this early? Spence. It must be him, calling about a rehearsal change or something. . .or something.

She felt a lazy smile spread across her lips as she reached for the bedside phone. "Hello?"

"Well, well, well. Did I get someone out of bed this morning?" a low voice questioned.

Lori's fingers turned to ice, and her heart seemed to stall. "What do you want?" she managed to whisper.

"Hardly a polite 'Good morning' for your father. Did I disturb you. . .or anyone else?"

Lori's stomach began to knot up. Why did she pick up the phone? Why did it have to be *him?* "I'm hanging up," she grated.

"Stop!" His voice was suddenly authoritative. "All right, princess, no chitchat. I'll get right to the point. Ted's son, John, has been asking about you. He's going to be in your neck of the woods this weekend. He'd like to see you." Her father paused for a moment. "He's promised to be on his best behavior."

So this was where things ended. Pay off the little lady and when things settled down, bring *him* back into the picture. Deep down she had suspected it all along. The daughter and son of the two most important political families, seeing one another would be a hot press item. . .excellent publicity. She felt thoroughly nauseous.

"Lori? Did you hear me? He'll be coming in this evening at . . .7:05. Have you got that? It's Gate 13 on—"

"I won't be here," she blurted out.

"Why not?" His voice was cool, foreboding.

"I. . .I have a rehearsal tonight."

"You're lying."

"I. . .," Lori desperately tried to push down the panic rising in her chest, cutting off her already labored breaths. What was she supposed to do? Running into their ever-faithful aide at the Regency was proof positive that they were indeed watching her.

"Listen very carefully," her father stated slowly. "John will be arriving at 7:05 at Gate 13. I expect a certain little blond with a red Corvette will be waiting there to pick him up."

Circling the loops of the phone cord tightly around her fingers, Lori chose not to answer.

"I'm sure you understand, princess. And if not—" He broke off threateningly. "Just remember my last little unanswered phone call. Let's not forget who pays the rent on your precious castle." There were several seconds of ominous silence before the line finally clicked.

Lori sat almost trancelike for several minutes until a pain in her hand caused her to glance down. The coiled cord was beginning to cut off the circulation to her fingers and they were turning a dull shade of blue.

Carefully unwinding the cord, she replaced the phone in its cradle and eased back down onto the bed. *Tonight at 7:05.* That only gave her—wait! What was she thinking? Bolting upright, she frantically tried to think of some place she might go. . .any place. The rehearsal had been a lie—they usually did not practice on Friday evenings and especially not this weekend since Spence would be getting ready to cut his tape.

The recording session! He had invited her to go on Saturday morning. If John was coming. . . . Lori began to feel the usual queasiness churning about inside her. Here again she sat, trapped, nowhere to go, no one to help her. A convenient pawn in her father's age-old game.

Flinging the sheets away from her, she stumbled into the kitchen with a lethargy whose source was not from a lack of sleep. Puttering around the countertop mechanically, she mused about how unpredictable life was. . .even cruel. To take her from a wonderful night like the previous one and send her hurtling headlong into this. Cruel, yet typical. Such was her life. She ought to be used to it by now.

Sitting down with a large mug of strong coffee, she jumped when the phone jangled again. *Forget it. The machine can take him this time.* The answering message barely registered as she strode over to it, prepared to turn down the volume so she would not have to listen to more of her father's pompous ravings.

The beep sounded, and just as her finger touched the volume slide a different voice caught her ear.

"Hello? Lori? This is Spence. I'm sorry if I disturbed your sleep, but—"

Lori snatched up the phone. "Spence?"

"Yeah. Good morning." She could almost hear his smile.

"And good morning to you." She desperately tried to shove all of the torrid events of the morning into a far corner of her mind. Amazingly, with Spence as a reason, it was fairly easy. "So, does the soon-to-be-famous songwriter have a cold this morning?"

"Nope. So far so good. Not even a late night dip in a chilly lake can put me down." Spence's warm tones sent a shiver down Lori's spine.

"That's good to know. So what's up?"

"Well, I was wondering if you'd like to take another stab at keeping me out late again tonight."

"What, are you kidding? You want another swim?"

"No, actually I was thinking of something more formal."

"Oh, let's see, miniature golf?"

"Nope. You want to keep guessing, or should I give you a hint?"

"You might as well tell me," she sighed. "My brain is not up for games this morning."

"Okay. Does an evening listening to the St. Paul Symphony Orchestra appeal to you?"

Lori felt the first relief of the morning. This could be her chance. "What time would that be?"

"The concert usually starts at 7:30, but we should probably leave here by 6:45 at the latest."

Perfect! "That sounds just fine. I'll even pick you up."

"Okay." There was a lingering pause. "Is everything okay, Lori?"

"Sure," she added a little too hastily. "Yes. Everything's just fine. . .now."

"All right." He did not sound very convinced. "Well, see you at quarter to seven then?"

"Prompt."

"I'm looking forward to it," he said quietly.

"Me, too." A rush of warmth flooded her cheeks and continued to envelop her whole being.

"See ya then."

"Bye."

Slowly replacing the phone, Lori let a determined smile play across her mouth. She almost felt like laughing. For once, she was about to outsmart her father. For the moment, anyway. Her heart felt amazingly light, and she realized she did not even dread what she knew would happen. It would have to come sooner or later and now she was ready. . .she could and would do it.

❧

Lori slammed the door behind Spence and, walking around the front of her car, slid into her own seat. She let her eyes wander over to him for the hundredth time since she had picked him up at his apartment. He definitely did justice to the black, trim tuxedo. Even his hair was neatly slicked down. . .all but that forever wayward cowlick on the right side of his forehead. She suppressed a giggle as she tried to push the curl away.

"It's no use," he informed her with a grin. "My mom even tried to cut it off when I was a kid. I had this half-inch spike, sticking straight out from my head. She left it alone after that."

Lori sighed with a smile as she gazed at him. "You know, you're quite handsome, Spencer Berg." Then she broke into a laugh as she finally noticed his bow tie peeking out from behind his shirt's tiny lapels. Rather than the customary black or white, it shouted its presence with a brilliant blue background covered with a variety of Hawaiian tropical flowers. The thing was positively garish.

"Where did you get *that*?" she gasped between spurts of laughter.

"You like it?" He smiled as he gently stroked the silky fabric. "Guess."

Lori rolled her eyes and grinned. "I think I know. Was it your mom?"

"Ah, you remember my piano tie."

"Your family must all be nuts," she said, starting the car. "I'd like to meet them sometime."

"I'd like that, too."

They drove for several minutes in companionable silence as

the radio softly played baroque from a local classical station.

"Say," Spence suddenly piped up, "I'm at the disadvantage here. You've never told me what *you* look like, you know."

"What?"

"Fair is fair."

Lori swallowed an uncomfortable lump in her throat. "Why do you want to know how I look? Is it that important to you?"

He was obviously puzzled at her question. "I. . .I don't know. I'm just curious, I guess. Isn't that okay?"

She suddenly felt foolish over her little outburst. "Sure," she tried to laugh lightly. "Let's see. . .Lori. I'm about five foot five. Never mind the weight. I have blond hair, green eyes, and a big mouth. Anything else you want to know?"

He sputtered into a chuckle. "No, I guess that about covers it in a nutshell." His voice dropped off as he faced forward for a quiet moment. "You know, Lori. You don't have to be self-conscious around me. I don't know if looks are a big deal to you, but in case you haven't noticed, I can't see you anyway."

Troubled, she avoided his face, yet knowing full well what he was saying. "I know," she stated simply. "And you'll never know how much. . .how much. . . ."

"How much what?"

"I don't know. I guess I'm just sort of glad you can't see me."

She signaled and turned off onto the exit that headed toward the Riverside Civic Center. Trying to erase the latest turn their conversation had taken, she concentrated on imagining the inside of the huge building. She had driven by the huge, gothic-looking auditorium often enough, but had never had the opportunity to go in. Settled right next to the river, the view from the rear terrace was stunning. If the interior was half as impressive as the ideal location, she knew she would not be disappointed.

"Do you come here often?" she asked.

"Mmm, once in a while. Corinne and I used to go quite regularly. But that was before my accident."

"Well," she said as she pulled into the elevated parking ramp, "I'm excited. I've never been to a symphony before." She carefully smoothed her black silk skirt as she emerged from the car and went around to Spence's side. After he had pulled himself out, she locked the doors and took his arm, habitually tucking his hand into the crook of her elbow.

"I think I'm going to wear a hole in your arm," he said with a smile.

"I don't mind. I have two."

They continued across the cement floor of the parking ramp. Lori did not know which she was feeling more excited about: the thought of seeing a live symphony or the fact that Spence was touching her arm. True, he had done it a lot now, but each touch seemed like a caress, and with each touch, the fluttering she felt in her heart grew stronger. It was a feeling she was unaccustomed to, and it fascinated her and frightened her at the same time.

❧

Spence let out a long breath as they waited in their plushly padded seats. Lori had been completely silent since entering the main floor of the auditorium. Every once in a while, he would catch a hint of a shiver traveling up her arm.

"Is it as beautiful as I remember?" he asked.

"It's gorgeous," she nearly whispered. "I just can't believe the. . .the. . .everything! You know, in a way, it looks a lot like Penny Lane—the chandeliers and touches of gold in the enormous moldings—but it's different. I think it's the people. You should see how some of these people are decked out. I'm sitting here feeling sort of like a frump."

"I hardly think you're a 'frump,' Lori," Spence chuckled.

"I guess it's just so. . .elegant. . .yet. . . ." She hesitated. "There aren't any words to describe it," she finally admitted.

Spence heard her draw in a deep breath, and he knew they were turning down the house lights by the dull blackness that layered over the meager glow he had sensed earlier.

Lori seemed to be shuffling with her program. "Hey," she whispered. "This is a baroque concert. Why didn't you tell me?"

"I wanted it to be a surprise." He grinned in her direction.

A round of applause went up from the audience, and Spence knew the conductor had arrived on stage. He eagerly held his breath awaiting the first number. It did not disappoint him. The lush sounds of strings, mandolins, harpsichords, and brass blended together in beautiful synchronism. These were the times he was glad, in a sense, that he could not see. There were no distractions, no visual interruptions. Just pure, unadulterated bliss. He relaxed and lost himself.

Intermission arrived far too quickly for his liking.

"Would you like to take a stroll?" he asked the still-silent Lori. "Stretch your legs?"

"No, thanks. I just like sitting here and taking everything in. Who knows when I'll have another opportunity like this."

"Well, I'll certainly take you again," he added. "Did you think this would be your last visit here?"

Lori cleared her throat. "Oh, no. I mean, I was just thinking that. . .never mind. I don't know what I meant."

Spence knew she was hedging about something. "Lori, are you planning on. . .going somewhere?" He was not sure why he asked, but he felt an inexplicable panic. It had almost seemed she had alluded to it, even though she had not said it aloud.

"No, no," she laughed. "Whatever gave you that silly idea?" But she lapsed into an uncharacteristic silence after that.

When the musicians reentered the auditorium and the lights were again dimmed, Spence leaned over to Lori. "Remember how you said that you couldn't really find the words to describe this place?"

"Yes," she said quietly.

"Do you know, that's how you are? Granted, I don't have the visual capabilities to try and describe you, but aside from that, you're a very complicated woman."

Lori remained very still.

"I want you to do something for me."

"What?" Her voice was barely audible.

"Read me the next piece that's on the program." He waited while she shuffled with the paper.

"It's Purcell. 'Second Movement: Adagio.' "

"And?"

"Um, 'Third Movement: Allegro from Sonata in D Major for Trumpet and Strings.' "

"Listen," he whispered close to her ear as the musicians tuned their instruments.

The first piece began, a slow, moving chorus of strings. "This is you," he breathed. "Quiet, mysterious. A bit sad." He let her listen to the remainder of the movement in silence.

Then the second portion began, a vast contrast from the first. Lively strings danced across the air and were soon joined by the triumphant sounds of a bright trumpet. "And this is you," he continued. "Joyful. Spontaneous, with this zest for life."

He felt her turning to face him. "You're as beautiful as this symphony, Lori. More. This is how *I* see you." There was no response. He reached out his hand to her bare arm and ran his fingers up her soft skin until he reached her hair, her face, gently caressing the delicate silkiness of her cheeks. They were wet. "Lori?" he murmured.

Her hands suddenly grasped his, almost desperately, and held them to her face and finally to her lips. Tiny sparks flew up his fingers and continued down his arm. Tenderly clasping his hands on each side of her face, he pulled her toward him until their lips brushed together ever so softly.

For a fleeting moment he remembered the night at his apartment. But, he realized as he placed his mouth on hers again, that kiss paled by comparison. There was something different now, something good, something beautiful. . .something infinitely better.

ten

I must be absolutely crazy, Lori thought as she drove home. Here she was, smiling her fool head off, and all the while tears were running down her cheeks. She tried to remember the last time she had cried. It had been long, long ago. . .before she had been empty. But these were a new kind of tears, ones she did not even know existed. She felt a strange sensation of joy and excitement and. . .things she could not quite describe.

As she turned off to the street leading to her condo, Spence's words kept echoing in her mind. No one had ever spoken to her that way, to tell her she was beautiful. . .comparing her to music. She shook her head. He was something else.

She was so wrapped up in her thoughts, she nearly didn't see the tow truck parked near the entrance of the underground security garage of her apartment complex. At first she paid it no mind, but gradually the realization began to hit her. This was Friday night. She glanced at her watch. Quarter after ten. Enough time for good old John to report back to Donald that his daughter had not shown. It was starting.

Braking just outside the garage door, she shut off the car and stepped out her door. She glanced over at the burly man in the truck who looked just a tad nervous. With quick steps she strode confidently over to his window, which he immediately rolled down.

"Good evening," she greeted the middle-aged man cordially.

"Uh, hi," he stammered as he shifted in his seat. He kept looking about, as if confused.

"Let me guess," Lori said. "Repo man?"

"Look, lady. I'm not sure what's going—"

"Oh, don't be embarrassed. Everyone's got a job to do. I'm

Lori Sommers. I imagine you're looking for my Stingray there." She pointed in its direction, strangely without the feelings of remorse she had anticipated.

He continued to stare at her in chagrin.

"Let's make one of your jobs easy tonight, shall we?" She gave him a winning smile, detached her car keys from her key chain, and extended her hand into the window of his pickup, unceremoniously dumping the keys into his lap. "Have a nice evening," she called over her shoulder as she headed for the front door of the complex.

Once inside her apartment, Lori could not resist smiling at the profusion of flashing lights on her answering machine. Her father must have driven himself into a frenzy, trying to reach her for the last several hours. The thought gave her a great deal of satisfaction.

Throwing her purse onto the sofa, she continued toward the machine and was about to shut it off when she had a new idea. She flipped up the lid and pressed the button to record a new outgoing message. The tape rewound slowly, and after a series of clicks and blinking lights, the telltale beep gave her the cue.

"Hello, you've reached Lori Sommers. I'm very sorry I've missed your call, but you see. . .the princess has vacated the castle. The king is on his own."

She pushed the button for emphasis and waited for the machine to replay her message. For the first time ever, she really hoped that he would call, because it would be the last time, the last time for a lot of things. And from now on, she would erase every image and every thought of Donald Jacobs forever.

Lori walked purposefully down the hall to pack her suitcase.

❧

"Is Lori here yet?" Spence asked Mike for the thousandth time that morning.

"No, not yet. Relax, Spence, it's only 9:30. Recording doesn't start for half an hour."

Spence sighed as he sat back down at the piano. She would come, he knew she would. Right now he should be concentrating on his music. He ran a couple of scales up and down the keys, followed with some arpeggios, and drifted into one of his favorite jazz melodies.

"You and your Joplin," a teasing voice said from behind him.

He smiled. "Any other requests?" he threw back, never even pausing in his notes.

"How about some Purcell."

He stopped and turned toward her. "I'm afraid after last night it would suffer by comparison."

"I think you're right," she agreed softly.

"Well, she's here!" Mike announced as he thundered into the studio. "Maybe we can start early, now that our virtuoso isn't biting his nails anymore."

"Be quiet, Mike," Spence said, smiling. "Go make yourself useful and see if Bruce is ready to start this thing."

"Sure, sure. I can take a hint."

"I'm glad you came," Spence said after Mike had left.

"Wouldn't miss it. Where should I go?"

"I think they'll let you sit in the control booth. Then you can hear everything."

"Okay. Break a. . .vocal cord." She laughed lightly, and Spence could hear her exiting the room.

"All righty, Spence." Bruce Simpson's voice came through the speakers. "Let's get this show on the road. Your headset's right in front of you."

Spence reached out, grasped the earphones, and slipped them on. "I'm gonna start with the country one."

"Whatever you want," Bruce agreed. "Just take her easy, relax. Have fun with this. Give us about ten seconds, then you just start whenever you're ready."

Lori watched through the heavy glass windows in anticipation. She could not imagine the thrill and the nervousness Spence must be feeling down there in the recording booth all alone.

After the allotted ten seconds had passed, she noticed him stretch out his hands. Unconsciously, she held her breath.

As his fingers brushed over the ivory keys, the simple, rustic melody poured out. She waited to hear the words that she had had only a taste of that day. When Spence's clear, strong tenor broke through the control room speakers, she shut out everything around her, closing her eyes to concentrate solely on all the hard work she knew he had put into the message of the song.

"She slipped her tiny fingers
into her daddy's great big hand,
studying the callouses
he'd earned from working land.
His farmer's touch was gentle
when he held his baby tight,
rocking her to sleep as he did
each and every night.
Some years later her world was torn
when Daddy was laid to rest.
She cried as she gently touched once more
those hands that crossed his chest.
The bottle that they'd often clutched
had closed this life's door,
but despite his imperfections,
she couldn't love him more.

"Oh, she'd loved the man
with the scars on his hands.
He was all she thought she'd need.
But then came the day
that had taken him away,
now what kind of life would she lead?
Where were those strong and loving hands?"

Lori's eyes fluttered open in confusion. What kind of a song was this? A song about some woman's daddy? The next verse started, and she tried to shove her thoughts back so she might concentrate again.

"She grew up and found a man,
a carpenter by trade.

Perhaps this was her second chance
after the price she'd paid.
The golden band slipped on easily
declaring her love so true.
His toughened hands held tight to hers
as he proclaimed, 'I do.'
A few years later she sat and wept
her husband now was gone.
It seems that golden band came off
as easily as it went on.
He'd gone and found another love
said the note upon the door.
She quietly closed up inside
she had no love anymore."

Lori swallowed a huge, scratchy lump in her throat. This was getting a mite strange. . .not to mention personal. She began to wonder if Spence knew something. No. That was impossible. No one knew.

"Oh, she'd loved the man
with the scars on his hands.
He was all she thought she'd need.
But then came the day
that had taken him away,
now what kind of life would she lead?
Where were those strong and loving hands?

"One night in desperation,
her thoughts in such a whirl,
she took down the book she'd had
when she was just a little girl.
Through her tears she read of Him,
the One Who died for all of man.
So that she might live again,
those nails had pierced His hands.

"Now she loves the Man
with the scars on His hands.
He's all she'll ever need.
There will never come a day
when He'll forsake her in any way.
Oh, what a life she can lead
because of His strong and loving hands!
She'd always love those hands."

Quiet chords brought the song to a close, but Lori barely noticed. She was too busy trying to find the way to the door through her veil of tears.

"Hey, Lori." She felt Mike grab her arm.

Blinking frantically, she began to wipe her eyes. "Oh, hi, Mike. Excuse me for a second. I think I've got something behind my contact. Could you direct me to the restrooms?"

"Sure. . .third door on the left, down the hall." He pointed her on her way. "Are you sure you're okay?"

"Fine, thanks." Lori managed a wobbly smile as her fingers curled around the door handle.

Inside the tiny restroom, she turned the cold water faucet on full force and repeatedly splashed her face, letting the stunning chill try to replace the cold that was gripping her soul. After several minutes, she dabbed at her face with a number of paper towels and peered into the small mirror.

Satisfied, she allowed herself a small smile. She had caught herself in time. No tears. And she was sure they were properly buried back where they belonged. But it had been too close. Those feelings seemed to be coming to a head far too often for comfort lately. And the only thread she could see linking those situations together was her new relationship with Spence.

"Serves you right," she muttered to her reflection. "You should have known better. To think it would be any different with someone like him." She threw the paper towels forcefully into the trash. "When will you learn. . .it's only you and no one else."

Glancing at her watch, she realized those few minutes had slid into fifteen. Spence was probably done with his other song by now. Sheepishly, she emerged from her sequestered place and wandered back down the hall toward the booth. She watched through the observation glass for a moment. They seemed to have wrapped things up. Spence and Mike were talking in the studio and Bruce was flipping a sequence of knobs and switches in front of him. Maybe it would be best if she just waited out here for them. Then it would not look so obvious, as if she had tried to miss the last song.

Out of the corner of her eye, Lori saw Mike heading in her direction with Spence close in tow. She took a deep breath just as they emerged through the door.

"You okay, Lori?" Spence's face registered concern.

"Yes, I'm fine," she said lightly. "Those finicky contacts, you know."

"So did you like the songs?" Spence asked.

"Excuse me." Mike dropped Spence's arm and headed back into the control room. "I'm gonna see if Bruce is doing the playback yet." He cleared his throat and left with a rather uncomfortable look on his face.

"Did you like them?"

"Hmm?" Lori swung her gaze back to Spence.

"The songs." His voice was starting to show an edge of impatience.

"Oh. Right. I heard the first one. It was really pretty. I loved the music. I honestly don't know how you come up with those melodies and—"

"I see."

They both shifted around in awkward silence.

"Did you hear the second song?"

"No, I'm sorry. My contacts were giving me problems. I sort of—"

"Will you excuse me for a second?" he broke in again.

"Sure," she said quietly. By this time she was beginning to feel guilty. Not to mention confused. *I seem to feel that a lot lately.*

Spence stepped back into the room where Bruce and Mike were busy listening to the replay. She watched them talk and occasionally laugh while she stood outside. Was she supposed to wait for him? Or had he excused himself for good? Chewing anxiously on her thumbnail, Lori glanced down the hall toward the door and then toward the men. He had not really said she should wait for him.

She took one last glance at Spence. He was waving his arms around animatedly, gesturing about something. Bruce and Mike broke into a hearty laugh. It reminded her of the night she ha•'d seen him outside his church, talking to that young woman. Once again, it rankled her. Why was it that she had yet to see that side of Spencer Berg? Why was it reserved for everyone but her?

With a look that mingled her feelings of frustration and helplessness, Lori started slowly down the hall. By the time she reached the door, she was going at a good clip. Okay, enough of hanging onto Spence's shirttails for now. If he wanted to find her, he could. In the meantime, she had other things to do. Like finding a place to live. She might try Maggie. Lori was pretty sure the older woman would not turn her away. Besides, it would only be temporary.

Now that things had come to a head with her father, her only choice was to move on. . .start over. . .again. Some place where he could not find her. That would take money. If she was creative with her meager salary from the theater, it might be enough.

Her thoughts were busy as she trailed along the streets and sidewalks of Minneapolis. She would miss this place. Ahead and slightly above her, a sign on the side of the street caught her eye; LAKE OF THE ISLES—5 BLOCKS EAST.

That special evening of crisp, night air, cool water, and warm caresses flooded over her. Deep, dark eyes challenging, yet accepting her. A lump grew painfully large in her throat. Despite how terribly she wanted to deny it, it was not the city she would miss at all.

❧

"Bruce, can I use your phone?" Spence tapped his fingers against the back of the chair he leaned on.

"Sure. Mike, you know where my office is. Take him on down."

"Thanks." Spence stood and waited for Mike's prompting hand.

On their way down the hall, Mike spoke up. "You'll probably think I'm butting in, but go easy on her, Spence. She didn't miss that song on purpose, you know."

Spence let out a huff of breath in doubt. "Contacts, eh?"

"Yeah, I know," Mike appeased. "She needs contacts about as much as you do. No offense."

They finally entered Bruce's office, and Spence heard Mike reaching for the telephone. He tried to grasp the receiver from his friend's hands, but Mike held onto it.

"Ease up, buddy. She had no way of knowing that second song was for her. You know she would have stayed otherwise."

Spence nodded impatiently, not wanting Mike to talk him out of his present mood. He had bared his all for the first time in a long while. . .only to be made a fool of. He deserved to feel dejected. "I just don't understand. Why did she have to—"

"Spence, look," Mike said firmly. "I don't know much about Lori. I don't think anyone does, actually. But I saw her face when she left the booth. She was hurting, man. Really hurting." He paused, as if to let his words soak in so Spence would get their full effect.

"Now don't get mad at me here," he continued. "But for once. . .let's lay aside your fragile ego and concentrate on why she left in the first place. You struck something pretty deep inside her. Now, if you care about her as much as you seem to, it's your job to find out what it was."

The anger and hurt that had been pushing against Spence's chest slowly deflated. He let his shoulders slump in a sort of forfeit. Mike was right. . .and he had been too selfish and prideful to see it. He nodded slowly and felt Mike's grip loosen on the phone.

"Gentle," he reminded Spence again. "Those lyrics of yours would get to anybody."

A crooked smile crept across Spence's face as Mike started to leave the office. "Thanks, Mike," he said quietly.

"Yep." Mike's quick footsteps started down the hall.

Fumbling momentarily with the buttons, Spence dialed the number that had stored itself in his memory after hearing it the first time.

He sat breathlessly through several rings and felt his heart sink as her machine answered the line. Expecting her usual message, his ears pricked at this new greeting.

"Hello, you've reached Lori Sommers. I'm very sorry I've missed your call, but you see. . .the princess has vacated the castle. The king is on his own."

"What?" Spence clicked the receiver down and dialed again only to be met by the same strange reply. What was going on here? Princess. . .castle. . .king on his own? The weird words stumbled around in his brain, defying any semblance of order, some logical explanation.

"Dear God, what is going on here?" Spence cried in confusion.

A brief snip of a conversation flickered in his mind. It seemed so long ago. . . .

"Nice car."

"This was a gift. . .from my dad."

"A Manor Suites condo, a classic sports car. . . . Is all this from Daddy?"

"Yes."

Slowly, painfully, everything started to fall into its horrid place. Her prolific reputation, her refusal to discuss her father . . .her hint of leaving.

An odd sense of fear and panic set into Spence's stomach as he slammed the phone down. "Mike," he yelled as loud as his voice could carry. "Mike, come on!"

He heard his friend's fleeting footsteps and his breathless voice at the door. "What? What's up?"

"Get me out of here. Now. We're going to the theater." Spence still was not positive he knew what was going on, but he had an idea. And he earnestly hoped he was wrong.

eleven

Lori sat on the edge of the stage, swinging her legs back and forth.

"Lori?"

"Yes, Maggie?" She turned slightly to face her.

"I'll be leavin' now. Do you want me to take your suitcase with me?"

"If you wouldn't mind. I'm just going to sit here a while longer. I should be along shortly."

"No problem." Maggie's round face beamed at her. "It will be ever so nice to have company around again. I do get lonely sometimes." She paused, and her twinkling blue eyes looked thoughtful for a moment. "I am really sorry about your lease fallin' through, though. A real shame."

Lori waved her hand. "Ah, no matter. I needed to find a new place to live, anyway. I really do appreciate your taking me in. Especially on such short notice."

"Think nothing of it. It's what the good Lord would have anyone do."

"Uh, right." Lori cleared her throat and began picking at the cracks between the stage floorboards. She wondered if this was such a good idea after all.

"Well, I better be gettin' on home." The large gray bun on top of Maggie's head bounced up and down as she nodded her head. "We'll see you later then."

"Right." Lori waved one last time before Maggie pushed through the heavy side door.

Alone again, Lori sighed deeply as she looked out over the empty auditorium. It did look a lot like the Civic Center. She frowned as she wondered if she would ever fit out there. . .as a spectator. She had always been the one on the stage, performing for everyone else, always under someone else's direction. The stage. . .her life. . .they were much the same.

A barely perceptible sound came from backstage, and she turned her head. But it was silent again. Her thoughts wandered back to the time when she had found Spence praying back there. It still confused her. She had never set much store by God. What had He ever done for her? In fact, why had He let all the things that had happened to her happen at all? What purpose could they serve?

"No, God," she whispered to darkened rafters. "If You're up there at all, You certainly haven't shown it."

Another muffled sound drifted upstage, and Lori whirled around, springing to her feet. "Who's back there?" she demanded, trying to exude some authority in her voice, rather than the fear that was making her knees shake.

One of the curtains moved and a figure stepped into the wings, slowly emerging onto the stage.

She let out a loud breath of relief at the sight of him. "Spencer Berg! What are you trying to do? Give me a heart attack?"

His face remained serious as he shook his head.

"So, what are you doing here?" she asked, perplexed by his unusual quietness, the odd expression he wore.

"I was going to ask you the same thing."

"Oh. I um, just came down to see Maggie. I sort of—"

"Needed a place to stay?" he finished for her.

"Yes. How did you know?" She looked at him suspiciously.

He shrugged his shoulders as he finally approached the center of the stage. "Not important." He continued forward until he came within several feet of her, facing her directly. "So, did you come here to rehearse by yourself?"

"No," she faltered slightly. "Just to think, I guess."

He did not speak for a few seconds. "Tell me again what you look like."

"What?" Lori was becoming bewildered by his line of questions. It was quite unnerving.

"What you look like," he repeated.

He took a step closer, and she reflexively took one back. At that instant she felt her heel teeter on the edge of the stage. Spence's hand shot out and grabbed her arm securely.

Her heart was racing uncontrollably as she glanced over her shoulder at the eight-foot drop. "What are you doing?" she snapped as she yanked her arm free of his grasp. At the same time she sidestepped and moved toward safer ground.

"Trying to get you to trust me." He had turned his body, obviously following the sound of her voice and steps.

"You certainly have a funny way of doing it!"

"I'm sorry if I frightened you. I was trying to make a point."

"And what would that be?"

"Things aren't always what they seem."

"Oh, brother. Psychology 101. Give me a break." She rolled her eyes as her arms folded in front of her.

Spence's face was still sober, his eyes intense. "Did you know how close you were to that edge?"

"Of course not! Why else would I have nearly fallen?"

"Did you wonder how *I* knew you were that close?"

"You're talking in riddles. And I have better things to do than to stand around here and wait for you to scare me *or* ask dumb questions!" She started toward the side stage steps, but again Spence intercepted her.

"Please wait." His voice was softer.

She tilted her head, narrowing her eyes. "Why? What exactly do you want from me, Spence?"

He dropped his chin to his chest for a moment before lifting it again. "I'm sorry, Lori. I was going to try and explain to you about the omnipotence of God, how He's everywhere. . .knows everything about us, but. . . ."

"But what?" She was suddenly curious.

"I can't."

"Why not?"

"Because you have to know yourself first."

Lori almost snickered at that response. "I think you sat too long in that cold lake water, that's what I think." She started to pull away again, but Spence never seemed to fail at finding her arm before she made it out of his reach.

" 'She walks in beauty,' " he said gently.

"What?" Her eyes roved back to his.

" 'She walks in beauty,' " he began again, " 'like the night of cloudless climes and starry skies; And all that's best of dark and bright meet in her aspect and her eyes.' "

"Byron," Lori acknowledged softly.

He gave a slight nod. "You're well-read. But there's more: 'Pay no mind the beauty that shines forth of her face, for this is only a start. Man looks at the outward appearance, but the Lord looks at the heart.' "

She stood, puzzled. "That's not Byron. At least not that last part."

"No," he said, grasping her hands. "That's Berg. With some help from the Bible."

"The Bible?"

"Lori," he sighed, "I've been trying to tell you all along that your appearance doesn't matter to me."

"Of course," she scoffed. "You can't see me."

"But," his voice remained tender, "it matters even less to God."

"God!" Lori yanked her hands away and threw them up in the air. "God! Don't tell me this face and this body don't matter to God. If He did create all things, then why did He make me look this way? Why?"

Spence drew in a deep breath as he closed his eyes. "Why do you hate the way you look, Lori?"

She tried to laugh, but it came out unnatural and tinny. "Why would you think that? My looks have gotten me more than you'll ever know!"

Spence was quiet for a minute, and when Lori finally dared to look at him, she thought she saw a trace of unshed tears, glistening in his eyes.

"Some of those things," he ventured, "I'm sure you didn't count on. . .or want. Did you?"

Lori grasped her stomach. She felt as though she had been hit hard. All of her breath and life were slowly draining out of her. "What do you mean?" she whispered.

"Come on, Lori. Don't close up on me. For once, let me in. I can take it. I can take your pain. You've got too much. . .let it out."

She tried to take a fortifying breath, but it did not come easily. "Don't be ridiculous," she said flippantly. The actress was back. "Who would have hurt me?"

"Lots of people. Some of them I know. Others I don't. Some people like maybe. . .your father?"

The fine, threadbare string that had been holding her together for seven years snapped. Short, gasping breaths wheezed out of her mouth. For the first time Lori felt real fear. . .fear of being vulnerable, open to wounds, of being known. Known truly for who she was.

Her mouth was dry and her insides were heaving at all the memories that had suddenly flooded out when Spence had broken the thin dam that held them in.

She wanted to run at him, beat him with her fists, scream that she hated him. But she didn't. She did the only thing she had ever known.

Curling her fingers into tight fists, she bolted toward the steps that should have been her retreat long before now. She had almost made it. It could have been so simple. The show would have ended, she would have left—gone to a new city. A place where no one would know.

The door spelled out her exit and she smashed against it, hoping to dislodge some of the heaviness hanging on her as well. Outside, she blinked her dry eyes in the blinding sunshine, totally oblivious to its warmth. She could see no sun, no light. . .only darkness, such as she had never seen before.

And she ran again.

❧

Spence plunked his coins into the bus's fare box and sat dejectedly in the nearest seat. He felt hollow and empty and nauseous, all at the same time.

His eyes began to burn again, and he pushed his glasses up the bridge of his nose. The habitual stops and starts of the bus were a blur on the surface of his consciousness. There seemed to be no time.

After an indistinct period, he heard the driver's polite voice. "This is your stop, mister." With wooden legs, Spence moved to the door, down the steps, and onto the sidewalk.

He found his apartment easily enough, but fumbling for his keys made him more agitated, and they fell to the floor.

Dropping to his hands and knees, he swept his hands across the musty carpeting of the hallway, hoping his fingers would make contact with the keys.

Down the hall, elevator doors opened and muffled footsteps headed toward him.

"Spence?"

He sighed wearily as he sat back on his knees. "Corinne," he whispered. "Please, help me."

Her slim arm came around his waist, and she helped pull him to his feet. He heard the key sliding into the lock and the welcomed sound of the door squeaking open. He fairly fell into the entrance and clambered over to the couch.

"Spencer," Corinne's voice held a familiar, motherly tone. "What is going on?"

"I'll tell you," he said breathlessly as his head flopped back against the couch. "I'll tell you. And then I need you to help me pray."

❧

How much time had passed, Lori did not know. It seemed light years since she had left the theater. She felt somehow detached from it all.

She held up the crumpled piece of paper and compared the number with the one on the small yellow house before her: 2406. Yep, this was Maggie's place. She traipsed up the well-kept walk toward the narrow steps.

Pausing with her finger near the doorbell, she debated

whether to ring or just walk in, or what? After all, she would be living here for a while. . .surely she would not ring the bell every time she came home.

A slip of paper tucked discreetly in the keyhole caught her eye, and she pulled it from its hiding place. A note from Maggie:

Lori,

Had to run to the grocery store. Be back in fifteen minutes.

Maggie

P.S. Spencer called a while ago.

Lori squashed the note in her shaking fist, pretending that she had not seen the last line. She jiggled the doorknob and sighed with relief when it turned easily under her touch.

She stepped into the small, dimly lit living room and glanced around. The home held the unmistakable smell of a. . . Grandma's house. Lori grinned as she recalled one of the few happy memories of her childhood. Visiting her mother's parents in Tennessee had always been a treat. She had been able to spend most of her summers at Grandpa and Grandma Kensington's horse ranch. Oh, how she had loved that place. The house always held the lingering scent of fresh bread and spices, and the barn had its own familiar, cozy smell of hay, saddle leather, and horse.

Lori wondered if her life might have been different had she been able to continue spending her vacations there. But, as with everything, her father had dominated, and the summer she had turned fifteen—the summer after the "incident"—her visits had stopped.

She imagined the visits had ended because she would have been too far away to "manage" and her father was afraid to have her surrounded by people who seemed to truly care for her, people who might have taken action had they found out about the "unfortunate incident."

Shaking off her melancholy, Lori meandered through the

short hallways, studying the quaint kitchen that appeared not to have changed since about 1955, the small, tidy bathroom, and the two bedrooms, both tastefully decorated with a unique assortment of antiques. The entire place held a definite homey feel, one that would take time to get used to.

Spying her suitcase on the pink, ruffled twin bed, Lori stepped into the smaller of the two rooms and flopped down on the quilted satin comforter.

One small window framed by white eyelet priscillas curtains provided her a view of the neighbor's eaves. She rolled onto her back and stared at the ceiling, wondering how long she would sleep in this bed. . .and where the next one might be.

She had never felt so empty. . .so alone. Tears slid out the corners of her eyes, trickling down toward her ears. She wiped at them in irritation. She had preferred it when she had not been able to cry.

With a heavy breath, she sat up and gazed vacantly toward the floor at the rose pattern in the area rug.

A click from the front door latch pricked her ears, and she shot a look toward the hallway. Was Maggie home already? No voice called out in greeting.

A flash of fear cinched her heart. . .the door had been open. Anyone could have walked in. She scanned the room in panic, looking for any place that might conceal her. No place! The room was barely big enough to hold the small bed and dresser.

Maybe underneath the bed. . .but by the time she had decided she might be able to squeeze under it, the footsteps were coming down the hall.

Lori gripped the side of the bed, bunching up the spread beneath her sweaty palms. She did not want to close her eyes, yet she did not want to face what might happen, either.

As the slow taps came closer, a terrifying thought raced through her mind. It had been long enough since she had left her apartment. . .long enough for her father to have heard her message. . .long enough for him to have hired someone to find her.

twelve

In her mind, Lori desperately raced through the house, trying to remember if there were any other exits. She thought she had seen a back door in the kitchen. . .but what if it was locked? Meanwhile, the deliberate footsteps sounded ominously on the hard, wooden floor. She heard whoever it was pause at Maggie's bedroom, then step inside.

Suddenly she remembered the layout of the house. Every room opened into the other in a continuous circle. If she could duck down the rest of the hall, through the kitchen, and get to the living room, the front door would be right there—she might make it. Another footfall. She stood abruptly. No, she *had* to make it.

Thankful that she had left her shoes on, she moved toward the door as silently as she could. Her heart, nearly in her throat, fluttered in terror as she dared a peek around the doorjamb.

The hall was empty. Whoever was here was still in Maggie's room. Lori willed her feet to move with each step as she snuck down the hallway. What she wouldn't give for a solid, carpeted floor right now. She hoped she would not hit any squeaks in the floorboards.

Not quite sure enough to reward herself with a deep breath, she stepped around the short section of wall that connected the hall and the door to the living room. Placing an unsure toe on the faded oriental rug, she nearly lost her footing when she heard the intruder continuing down the hall. To think there was only one thin wall between them, unnerved her.

She earnestly hoped he would stop and peruse her room as well. It would be her only chance to wrench open the front door and run as fast as she could.

Not taking more time to contemplate the situation, she resumed her flight and felt her heart lift slightly when she saw the door had been left open. The intruder had not locked it behind himself.

No longer concerned about noise, Lori rushed the last several feet, flung open the screen door, and leaped down the steps, landing on the lawn.

About to continue her sprint down the sidewalk, Lori saw Maggie's car approaching. Running into the street, her arms flailing wildly, Lori managed to get Maggie to stop. Running to the passenger side, she hopped in. "Go!" Lori said, nearly out of breath.

"What?"

"Go!" She jabbed her finger in a forward direction, and thankfully, Maggie complied. . .but only after both of them saw the tall, blond man standing at the foot of the steps.

When they had driven several blocks, Maggie ventured a glance toward Lori. "What is going on?" Her normally jovial face was creased with concern and worry.

"I. . .I don't exactly know," Lori lied. "It seems as though that man broke into your house."

"Where were you?"

"In the bedroom."

Maggie concentrated on her driving, shaking her head slowly."I don't believe it. It's always been such a peaceful neighborhood."

Lori took a moment to rub her temples and then the spot above her knee that must have been bumped on her way out the door. "I guess there's always a first time."

"Well," Maggie said as she reached over and grasped Lori's hand, "I just thank God that you got out all right."

Lori nodded, silent.

"Did you get a good look at him?" Maggie inquired.

"The same as you, I think."

"Good. Because we're heading to the police department right now."

Lori almost shook her head to argue, but decided against it. Wanting to keep the whole incident a secret would generate more suspicion. Let Maggie file her report. If the man had been sent by her father, they would never find the guy anyway. She knew that for a certainty. Her father always covered his tracks too well.

❧

"Well, Mrs. Dempsey, Miss Sommers," the tall, dark-haired sergeant said as he rounded his desk. "It doesn't seem that any damage has been done to your home. He apparently left soon after you did." He raised his eyes from the reports. "You've stated that neither of you recognized the man, but do you know anyone who might have had him follow one or both of you?"

Maggie shook her head and followed the police officer's gaze to Lori. She glanced down and quietly shook her head as well. A shadow of doubt crossed Sergeant Malone's face as he continued to study her, but he eventually looked away.

"In any case," he continued, "it would be best if the two of you found somewhere else to stay for a few days. We'll keep an eye on the place and make sure new locks are put in. Okay?"

"Thank you, Sergeant." Maggie jumped to her feet and grasped his hand. "You're doing a wonderful job here."

"Thanks," he said as an easy smile came across his face. "You two just be careful. . .nothing foolish, okay? No going anywhere alone, that sort of thing."

Both women nodded their assent.

After stepping out into the bright sunshine, the two women stared at each other.

"Well," Maggie broke the silence, "what do we do?"

"Let's get a hotel room," Lori offered. "I'll pay. It's the least I can do after the mess I've caused you."

The older woman frowned slightly. "Lori, it wasn't your fault my house was broken into."

Lori gulped and fixed her eyes across the street. "Oh. . .I just meant. . .well, you'd offered to take me in and this just happened and. . .just let me do this, okay?"

"But where will you get the money for a hotel?"

"I have money." Lori inwardly grimaced when she thought of dipping into her little nest egg. That had been her means of getting out of here. Now this. . . . It seemed good old Donald Jacobs was forever popping up, full of unexpected surprises. And to think she honestly thought she had started to beat him.

They checked into a double suite at a nearby hotel and spent the afternoon settling in and putting away the few clothes they had been allowed to return for. Even while they were collecting their few personal things, policemen were milling about the house, dusting for prints and looking for any other clues that might lead to the mysterious intruder.

"I'm just so relieved that you weren't hurt," Maggie kept reiterating as they drove back to the hotel. "It's just so odd. . .I mean, he didn't touch anything in the house."

Lori merely nodded. She had decided earlier not to inform Maggie or the police that he had gone through her suitcase. Things had been neatly replaced, but he had neglected to close it and set it back on the floor.

When the supper hour came, neither of them felt like going out, so they ordered hamburgers from room service.

"It's kind of nice not to have to go to rehearsal tonight," Lori commented as she finished wiping her fingers.

"Agreed," Maggie said before she finished her last bite. "By the way, Lori. Where is your car?"

"Oh, it's um. . .having some problems. It's probably being looked at right now. I'm not sure when they'll be done with it."

"That's too bad. Car troubles can be such a nuisance. Well,

we can take my old car wherever we need to go. It may not be sporty, but it still gets me places."

Lori smiled kindly at her friend. Maggie had not even so much as flinched when Lori had rattled off the car problem story. This woman seemed to trust her no matter what she said. It seemed awfully naive, yet refreshing, too. . .even though lying to the woman did cause a twinge of guilt.

❧

Spence emerged from his bedroom on Wednesday morning, feeling marginally better than he had since Saturday. He had canceled rehearsals for a few days, despite the fact that opening night was coming up just next week. He was confident everyone knew their parts, and his mind had been so frazzled he hardly believed that his direction would have been a help to anyone. Besides, they all seemed relieved by the break.

As he moved to the kitchen for his morning coffee, he thought about the disturbing telephone call he had received from Maggie on Saturday evening. He still found it hard to believe that someone had actually broken into her home. . .and while Lori was there! He silently thanked the Lord for at least the hundredth time that she was unharmed.

Spence slurped his scalding coffee and decided to forgo his usual bowl of cereal. He did not have much of an appetite. His mind kept reeling from the incident with Lori to his upcoming appointment that morning with Dr. Greene and the specialist. Corinne should be arriving shortly.

He dumped the rest of his coffee into the sink and headed for the shower. Just as he was about to enter the bathroom, the telephone jangled. He sighed, debating whether to pick it up or not. He decided he had better—it might be Corinne. . .or maybe—no, *she* would not call, not after their last encounter.

"Hello?"

"Hello. Is this Spencer Berg?" an unfamiliar man's voice asked.

"Yes, it is."

"Mr. Berg, my name is Jordan Kramer from The Way Music Corporation. We just wanted to let you know that we received your tape and well, frankly we were quite impressed."

Spence's breath caught in his chest. A smile was trying to crease his cheeks, but he was too much in shock to give it free rein.

"Mr. Berg?"

"Yes," he replied quickly.

"We are willing to offer you a writing contract."

The smile was fully in place, and Spence tried to unravel his tongue in order to respond. This was what he had been wanting his whole life.

"Mr. Berg?"

"I. . .I'm sorry," he stammered in the midst of a laugh. "I guess I'm just sort of in shock."

"No problem," Jordan Kramer's voice chuckled. "We'll send up the necessary papers to Bruce Simpson's studio, and he'll contact you when he receives them. We're looking forward to having you here."

"Here?" Spence echoed.

"Uh, yes. Most of our writers live in the area right around Nashville. Is that a problem?"

"Oh, no, no. I guess I knew that. I just still can't quite believe this is happening." He laughed again at his ineloquent stammerings. "Good thing you didn't conduct a phone interview with me, huh?"

"Right," Kramer agreed good-naturedly. "Well, God bless you, brother. We'll see you soon."

"You, too. And thank you. Thank you so much."

"You earned it. You've a special gift. You take care."

"You, too." Spence hung up the phone and felt like flying across the room. All else was forgotten. "Thank You, God," he shouted jubilantly as he clenched his fists in victory.

"Spence?" Corinne's voice came from the doorway.

He had not heard her enter.

"Spence! Aren't you ready yet? We have to be there in a half-hour. Go get in the shower!"

"Good morning, dear sister of mine." He grinned as he found his way over to her and proceeded to lead her in an awkward waltz around the room until both of them tumbled into the couch in laughter.

"What is wrong with you, Spencer?" she asked between giggles. "This is the happiest I've seen you in I don't know how long."

"I'll tell you why," he stated as he jumped to his feet and stuck out his chest proudly. "You, little sister, had just better start treating your big brother with some new respect. Then, when you hear one of my songs on the radio, you can tell your friends you're in good standing with your famous, song-writing brother." He waited for her reaction but there was only silence. "Hello? Corinne?"

"You're kidding," she whispered.

"Nope," he said gleefully.

"Spence!" she shrieked as she flung herself into his arms. "You did it! I knew you would!"

They held each other for several minutes until Corinne pushed him away. "Well, let's get going," she said shoving him toward the bathroom. "We'll see if we can top this day at the appointment. Now, go!"

Spence let the warm spray wash over him. Never had he felt so exuberant, so full of life. . .except for that small portion of his heart that he hadn't even known existed until Lori stepped into his life.

Now he would be leaving. . .for good. He did not know if he had ever consciously thought that she would go with him, but he had entertained ideas and fancies. Ones he probably shouldn't have. Look where they got him. They had taken him from being friends with her to something less than an acquaintance. . .a cool acquaintance at that. He and his pompous urgings, thinking he could fix the world and all its problems.

"Admit it, Spence," he muttered as he stepped from the shower. "A songwriter you may be, but an expert on human relations, no."

He padded to his room, changed into his jeans and shirt that he had laid out, and took a few moments to try and regain the expression he had been wearing when he left Corinne. This was a day he should be rejoicing and anticipating. And in a sense he was. . .except for that one part. It was the first time he had felt so passionately about anything or anyone, including his music. And it grieved him to know that the hurt he felt might never go away.

❧

Spence shifted around on the cold, hard examining table. The pungent odor of antiseptic mingled with a variety of other hospital smells, and he began to wish he had eaten some breakfast.

"Corinne?" he whispered.

"What?" she hissed back.

"What are they doing?"

"Well, they're in a huddle down the hall, looking at some charts—some of those funny pictures they took of your eyes after the accident—and. . .just sort of generally standing around."

His shoulders rose and fell with a heavy sigh. "When are they going to come and talk to us?"

"Be patient, Spence."

"Yeah, right." He curled his lip at her in a half-smirk.

"You know Mom's got half the population of Duluth praying for you right now," she reminded him.

Two sets of footsteps sounded in the tile-lined hall.

"Hold your breath, bro. Here they come." Spence could hear

his sister shifting in her chair as well.

"Spencer," Dr. Greene greeted him in a friendly tone. She grasped his hand and squeezed it tightly. "How have things been going?"

"Oh, you know," he said flippantly. "The usual run-of-the-mill stuff. Hang gliding, art class, race car driving." He was rewarded by her bubbly laughter.

"I warned you, Dr. Bray."

"So I see," laughed the older gentleman. He, too, pressed his hand into Spence's. "Good to finally meet you, Mr. Berg."

"Spence."

"Fine, Spence," the doctor agreed. "Well, let's have a look at your eyes, shall we?"

"Be my guest." Spence felt Dr. Bray's fingers gently parting his eyelid as he shone a light directly into his eye.

"Now, Dr. Greene says that you can sense changes in light and darkness. Correct?"

Spence nodded.

"To what degree?"

"Usually only extreme changes. Like now when you shine it right into my eye. It's not so evident if you opened or closed a curtain or something."

The doctor continued to turn Spence's head, seemingly studying him from all angles. When his hands dropped, Spence heard a pen scratching across paper in quick movements.

Taking yet another controlled breath, Spence wondered if he might explode before anyone spoke again.

"Spence," the elder doctor began, "Dr. Greene and I feel you would make a good candidate for the type of surgery we've discussed."

For the second time that day, Spence could not keep an impish grin from tweaking his lips.

"But," Dr. Bray began, "I want to make it very clear there are no guarantees with this. The scarring you've received on your corneas is minimal compared to some I've seen, yet a lot worse than others."

"Thanks, Doc," Spence joked. "You really know how to build a guy up."

The doctor chuckled as well. "Just want to be up front with you. Okay?"

"Sounds good." Spence wondered what Corinne's expression was about now.

"So," Dr. Greene interrupted, "we'd like to schedule you for next Tuesday morning, if that's all right."

"Tuesday?" Spence asked incredulously.

"Is that a problem?"

"Well. . .it's just that my show opens on Wednesday, but. . ."

"Oh, I'm truly sorry, Spence," Dr. Greene sympathized. "But Dr. Bray will be here for only a limited time before he leaves for another hospital in Ohio. Is there any way someone could fill in for you?"

Spence sighed in thought, then let out an easy smile. "Sure. There are plenty of capable people down there. Tuesday it will be. . .as long as I get to attend at least one performance!"

"Assured," Dr. Bray promised. "Maybe even two."

Spence held out his hand. "Thanks a lot, Doc."

"Don't thank me yet," he said, taking Spence's hand.

"Oh, but I will. I'll thank you now," Spence grinned, "and again when I can see your hand to grab it!"

thirteen

Lori sat at Maggie's small dining table, slowly sipping her mug of coffee. She threw one more glance over to the window above the sink, hoping the scene outside would have changed. Nope, still dark gray and rainy. Figured. It about matched her mood.

She sighed as she lifted the steaming beverage to her lips, vaguely aware of the puttering sounds coming from the bathroom.

"Are you sure you won't come to church with me?" Maggie asked as she poked her head into the hallway.

Lori shook her head. "No, thanks." She nervously traced the rim of her cup with her forefinger. "Maybe next week."

Maggie nodded in understanding before ducking back into the bathroom.

Next week. If everything went according to her plans, Lori would not be here the following Sunday. . .no more excuses to come up with. The musical would debut Wednesday night and run through Saturday. Then she was free to go. But where?

She quickly tried to review what was left of her small bundle of cash. Staying at the hotel for three nights had stripped it considerably. She would not be able to go as faraway as she had liked. . .but away it would be.

"Well," Maggie said as she breezed into the kitchen, "I don't mind telling you that it makes me a little more than nervous, leaving you here alone."

"Don't worry about me," Lori waved her aside. "Remember, there are all new locks and dead bolts on the doors."

The older woman still looked skeptical as she opened the back door leading to the small garage out back. "Keep things closed up. . .and don't go out alone!"

Lori snapped a rigid salute. "Yes, ma'am!"

A twinkle shone in Maggie's light blue eyes as she studied Lori for a moment. "It's good to have you here," she admitted in a quiet voice. "I hope you can stay for a while."

A lump began to form in Lori's throat, and she averted her gaze to the window. "Don't forget your umbrella." She waited until the door had closed before she rose to lock it.

As she watched Maggie scurry down the slick sidewalk, Lori almost wished she could stay, too. But growing fond of places or people was something she wouldd have to get over.

Twisting the heavy lock into place, she stared at it in contempt. *It seems I'm forever locked in somewhere. Too bad it's not as easy to lock out my father.*

Lori puttered around the house for the next several hours, desperately trying to find something to do. Maggie did not have a television, and the few books and magazines that were in the house seemed to have a religious theme to them. Lori attempted to read a few of them, but her mind just refused to comprehend much of it. . .or blocked it out. The content was familiar—basically everything she had heard during her vacations with her grandparents.

But although she vaguely remembered some of the Bible passages—"promises" as Grandma Kensington called them—most of them lost their significance after. . .well, after that night.

So, she contented herself with studying a United States map in the atlas, trying to figure out where her money might take her. Colorado seemed appealing.

Just before noon, Lori heard Maggie reentering the kitchen and walked out to meet her, eager for some company after the long morning. "Hi, how was church?"

"Wonderful." Maggie shrugged out of her damp raincoat and tugged at her scarf. "Still wish you would have come. Spencer was there. He asked about you."

"Hmm."

"Lori?" Maggie turned around to face her. "Not that it's any of my business, but. . .is there something going on with you and Spencer?"

Succeeding at not letting her gaze drop to the floor, Lori gave a half-hearted smile. "You're right, it's not your business. But, no, anyway." She turned and began rummaging through the refrigerator. "What do you want for lunch?"

"We prayed for him today."

With her back still turned, Lori rolled her eyes. Apparently Maggie did not consider the subject closed yet. "Really?" she asked, trying to sound polite instead of overlyinterested.

"He's having surgery on Tuesday."

"Surgery?" Lori tried not to whirl around too fast.

"Yes." Now, it seemed it was Maggie's turn to be coy as she nonchalantly began setting the table.

"What kind of surgery?"

"His eyes. They're going to try some new type of thing with corneal transplants."

"Will that bring back his eyesight?" Lori's voice was barely above a whisper.

Maggie shrugged. "Don't know. No guarantees, I guess. But we're all praying anyway."

Lori merely nodded and finished helping with the table. Yet all through lunch she could not keep her mind from reeling over this latest information. Spence. . .being able to see. That would make everything so. . .so different. He had been the only person around whom she could be herself. There was no pressure to look good, no expectations, but now. . . .

Maybe the operation would not work. A pang of guilt shot through Lori. Who was she to wish such a thing on anybody, especially Spence? If anyone deserved things to go well, he was the one. He was just so. . .good.

Besides, she reminded herself, by the time he would be up and around, the musical would be done and she would be long gone. He could go on to live his life completely once more, without her to mess things up for him. She unconsciously nodded. Things would be better all the way around.

"Oh," Maggie exclaimed, bringing Lori's attention back. "I almost forgot. He also heard from that music company. They've offered him a writing contract. I guess he'll be leaving for Nashville soon after *Brigadoon* is done."

Lori stared at Maggie. "That's great." She smiled weakly as she stirred her fork among her salad greens.

"Indeed. That boy has so much God-given talent. He'll change lives through his music, I know he will."

Lori nodded, pushed away from the table, and carried her bowl to the sink. "If you'll excuse me, I think I'm going to take a nap for a while."

"Are you feeling okay?" The older woman's broad brow furrowed in concern.

"Yeah. Just still trying to catch up from those nights in the hotel, that's all."

Plodding to her room, Lori lay on her bed and tried to understand why *her* leaving had not seemed half so bad as the thought of *Spence's* leaving. Emptiness gnawed within her. And it seemed to be after her very soul.

❧

Tuesday morning found Spence lying in his bed, much too eager to sleep. His mind was in such whirl, he could not pick out one thing and remain focused on it.

Rehearsals had resumed Monday. Everyone seemed genuinely happy over both of his bits of news. Between Mike, Tom, the stage manager, and several of the key cast members, Spence was fairly sure the show would come off just fine. Yet he could not help feeling the slightest twinge of regret. This was the last production he would be involved with at Penny Lane, and the thought of missing any of it bothered him.

Besides, the one thing he had wanted to do was to try and talk to Lori—at least to get things semi-patched up. But she was never available. Rehearsal came and went without a hitch, yet as soon as it was over, she was nowhere to be found. Well, at least he could take a hint.

❧

Spence shifted for what seemed like the thousandth time. If

there was one thing he would never get used to, it was a hospital bed.

"I can't wait to see you again," a slightly off-key bass voice sang out heartily.

"Knock it off, Kevin," Spence laughed at his older brother. "You're gonna make the patients sick."

"Quite right," Evelyn Berg agreed as she tucked the stiff sheets more tightly around Spence. "There might be people sleeping."

"Yeah, Kev," Corinne threw in. "Start acting your age—"

"Not your IQ," the remaining siblings joined in as they finished their childhood chant.

Spence knew the anesthetic that had just been administered was taking effect, but he was positive the joy he felt was from the nearness of his family. With a sleepy smile, he leaned back against his pillow. "I still can't believe you're all here."

"We'd be nowhere else, little brother," his sister, Tracy, answered.

"Mommy?" Spence recognized the voice of Molly, Tracy's four-year-old daughter. "Aren't we going to pray for Uncle Spence?"

"Yes, honey. I think we are."

A clamor of delight came from Justin and Ricky, Kevin's two rough-and-tumble boys, as they pounced to the bedside, eager to lay their sticky hands on their uncle as well.

"Well, Dad?" Spence asked. "You wanna show your stuff?"

"I certainly do," came his father's eager reply. "Kevin and Theresa, Corinne, you take that side. Tracy and Bob, you stand here by Mom and me."

Spence felt every pair of hands on him, and then his father's rough, house-painter hands tightly clasped his own.

"Father God," Marcus Berg began, "I lift up to You my son, Spencer. We want to thank You for the blessing he's been to our family, the unique person You've made him to be. Today, with hopeful hearts, we raise to You this surgery. We pray that Your Will be done in this matter.

"We trust You to guide the doctor's hands and to keep his mind sharp.

"Give Spencer a peace throughout the remainder of this time, into the recovery period. And a willing acceptance of whatever the result may be. . .trusting that in all things, Your Will be done. Thank You for providing this opportunity for him. In Jesus' name, we pray. Amen."

A chorus of amens filtered through Spence's growing drowsiness, and he tried to return the gentle squeeze of his father's fingers. "Thanks, Dad."

"Uncle Spence?"

"Yeah?" He grinned at Molly's sweet, lollipop breath, inches from his face.

"When you get well, you're going to watch me do my ballet. Okay?"

Spence nodded and returned the kiss she smacked on his lips.

"Okay, Mr. Berg," he heard a nurse say. The wheels began to squeak as the bed jerked into motion. "Off we go."

Kevin's call, "Go get 'em, little buddy!" was the last fuzzy thing he heard.

❧

Lori gripped the phone receiver while she waited for the ringing on the other end to cease.

"Hello?" a crackly voice answered.

Lori fought every urge within her to slam the phone back down. *Get a hold of yourself, girl.* "Hello. . .Grandma?"

There was a lingering silence before the woman answered. "Lori?" The response came on a shaky note.

"Yeah, Gram. It's me."

"Oh, child." Tears filled her voice. "It's been years."

Lori resisted some weepiness of her own. "I know. Almost eight years."

"Are you back in Tallahassee?"

"No. I'm in Minneapolis."

"Minnesota?" Grandma's reply was incredulous. "Aren't you freezing?"

"No, Gram," Lori laughed. "They have summer here, too."

"Well. Are you coming to visit us? Is that the reason for this pleasant surprise?"

"I'd love to, but. . . ," Lori swallowed painfully, "I can't."

"Sweetie, why not? Grandpa and I have missed you so much. You could come and ride again, just like you used to. I'm afraid Tariq is living out the remainder of his life in the pasture, but we have several other horses I know you would just love. I think Flash and you would get along just splendidly."

Oh, please don't make this harder than it already is, Lori thought. "I'm sorry. I just really don't know when I'll be down near Tennessee. My drama and all."

"Lori," Grandma asked quietly, "why did you quit coming to visit us?"

Lori's eyes shot up toward the ceiling as she pressed her lips tightly together. *You will not cry. You will not cry.* "Oh, you know, Grandma." She tried to sound flippant. "Teen-age girls get interested in other things."

"That doesn't sound like you."

Lori sighed in resignation. She should have known better than to try and pull one over on the woman who knew her better than anyone else. "Well, I really should go. Tell Grandpa hello from me, okay?"

"Lori, won't you come and see us? We've so often wondered what happened when you stopped coming here. I talked to your mother the other day, and she so rarely even mentions what you're doing."

"Yeah, well, I don't talk to them a whole lot."

"Do you want to see us?"

"Yes, Gram," Lori closed her eyes and nodded. "I do want to see you."

"Then the Lord will make a way for it to happen."

Yeah, right. The Lord. If He had been doing His job, I never would've had to stop coming to see them. "Sure. I really have to go now. Take care, Grandma."

"And you, Lori. We love you, you know."

Lori's hand trembled as she replaced the receiver in its cradle. *We love you, you know.* She had forgotten how good those words could sound. If only there was some place left in her heart for them to live.

fourteen

Lori clutched the wrapped package against her chest as she walked down the brightly lit halls of St. Luke's Hospital She had never liked hospitals, and the reason for her visit today did not help her uneasiness any.

Surveying the numbers next to each room door, she almost regretted it when she spotted the number the woman at the information desk had given her. Sure enough, BERG was neatly printed on a card beneath it. The door was closed. Maybe he was sleeping. She really should not bother him if he needed his rest.

As she turned to leave, a low murmur of voices drifted out from his room. Staring at the door handle, she debated her position. It was now or never. She would always live with a certain guilt if she did not apologize for her behavior that day on the stage. And she was fairly certain he would not push the subject again. . .or at least she hoped so.

Steeling her courage, she pushed the paddle on the door until it swung open. A dozen or so faces turned toward her. Her eyes flared in surprise. For some reason she had expected to find Spence with perhaps just a nurse. Who were all these people?

Once again thinking it might be best to leave, she began backing out the door. Barely aware of the quiet whispering, her feet were on their quick backtrack when she heard Spence's unmistakable voice. "Lori?"

She froze, afraid to look up.

"Come on in," Spence invited.

Her eyes slowly rose to meet the curious stares of the onlookers, who by now she had guessed to be his family. A partial wall blocked any view of Spence. Somehow she found her voice. "I. . .I'll come back later."

"Lori," came his teasing command, "get in here, will you?"

Managing a shaky smile, Lori stepped forward until she was past the partition. She cleared her throat quietly and wished in earnest that she had dressed up somewhat. Jeans, a rather old tee-shirt, no makeup, and hair slicked back into a ponytail was hardly the first impression she had wanted to give Spence's family.

"Hi, Spence." For the first time, she had gotten a good look at him. He was sitting up in bed, looking virtually the same, with the exception of the huge white bandages covering each eye, held in place with several rounds of gauze.

By his side stood a dark-haired young woman, close to Lori's age, who seemed to be a feminine version of Spence. Lori guessed she was Corinne.

"Well," Spence smiled as he shrugged his shoulders, "you said you wanted to meet my family someday."

Lori glanced around and found several of them smiling at her in a friendly manner. *He couldn't have told them too much about me.*

"Okay, guys. This is Lori Sommers, my star at Penny Lane."

"Hi," she said, blushing at Spence's description.

"Now, I can't see where you're standing, so introduce yourselves," he informed his entourage.

"Well, I'm Evelyn Berg, Spence's Mom." The petite woman stepped forward and grasped Lori's hand warmly. Her hair was the same shade as her son's, with streaks of gray running through it. "And this is my husband, Marcus."

Her husband, in turn, shook her hand and grinned, sporting the identical dimple that graced Spence's right cheek. Lori was astonished at the resemblance between the two men.

"I'm Corinne," said the young woman across the bed, smiling.

Lori nodded. "Spence has talked a lot about you."

"I'll bet." She smirked while giving her brother a playful smack on the arm.

"And I'm Tracy." Lori met the blue-eyed gaze of the woman who bore more similarities to her mother than the rest of the family. "This is my husband, Bob. My daughter, Molly." She tapped the blond little girl on the head.

"Hi, Molly." Lori smiled as she bent over toward the charmer.

"Hi!" Molly retorted. "You're pretty!"

A burning warmth raced across Lori's cheeks once more as the small crowd of people laughed.

"Hi, Lori." A taller, older version of Spence leaned over and pumped her hand emphatically. "You know, you're a whole lot prettier than Spence said you were."

"Kevin!" The tall brunette next to him nudged him with her elbow. "Theresa," she informed Lori. "And these are our sons, Ricky and Justin."

Each of the boys smiled shyly at her, but Lori could see that definite sparkle of mischief playing about their dark brown eyes. The same look she had seen in Spence's eyes occasionally.

"This is my crew," Spence added. "I told you they were all nuts."

"Really, Spencer," his mother admonished with a smile. "Let the poor girl find out for herself."

Several seconds of silence ensued while all of them looked at each other.

"So. . . ," Spence remarked.

"Well, see you later, bro." Corinne bent over and placed a kiss on his forehead. "Nice to finally meet you, Lori."

"You, too." Lori noticed Corinne quietly nudging the others along with a pointed glance as she left Spence's bedside. A deep warmth and appreciation for her grew in Lori's heart. His sister seemed to know the two of them needed to be alone.

"We'll come back this afternoon," Evelyn promised as the

others dutifully filed out in front of her.

After the door had closed, Lori studied Spence for some time. He looked so vulnerable. The desire to reach over and gently caress his face, his forever cowlicky hair, was almost overpowering. She wondered what to say.

"Opening night tonight," he commented, much to her relief.

"Yep."

"Nervous?"

"Nah. We'll pull it off. Even without our star director. Congratulations, by the way. I understand you're going to be a famous man."

He shrugged. "Famous, I don't know. Doing what I love, yes."

"I hope you'll be happy," Lori said as she gazed out the window, pondering his words. This was going to be a lot harder than she had thought.

"How's Maggie?"

"Fine. She'll be coming to see you tomorrow. She was pretty busy with last-minute costume stuff today."

"Sure wish I could be there."

"Can you? I mean, for even one of the performances?"

"I think so. Maybe Friday. For sure, Saturday. They couldn't possibly keep me away from that one."

Lori bit her lip to keep from asking the question uppermost in her mind. . .how the surgery had gone. He probably would not know yet anyway. And to be truthful, she really did not want to know. Spence seemed to know her too well already, and the thought of his deep brown eyes probing hers for further answers scared her.

"So I understand you'll be heading to Nashville. That'll be exciting. Tennessee is a beautiful state."

"You've been there?" His face turned toward her.

"Oh, yeah. My grandparents own a horse ranch there."

"Really? You'll have to come and visit me the next time you're down to see them."

"Oh. . .well, I don't see them too often. In fact, it's been quite a few years since I've been anywhere near there."

"I see."

His vague comment bothered her. And when she looked his way, he seemed distracted, as if his thoughts had drifted elsewhere.

"So, what do you do for fun? I mean, now that you're strapped to this comfort machine." She patted the bed.

"No kidding," he chuckled wryly. "Fortunately, I'm only stranded here until tomorrow. After that I have my free rein of the room or halls or whatever. Corinne has been coming in and reading to me sometimes so I don't go stir crazy."

"Oh, I brought you a present," she said, just then remembering the package clutched in her hands. "It's a CD of Purcell. A new one. . .a really great symphony, all digitally recorded and everything."

"Thanks." He grasped the gift as she held it out to his hands. "I'm sure it will bring back some pleasant memories."

Lori fidgeted with the end of her ponytail, twisting it around her finger. "Um, what were you reading? Maybe I could do that for a while." At least that would take the pressure off from trying to come up with conversation. She searched the surrounding tables for a book, but could not see one anywhere. "Is the book still here?" When he did not answer, Lori lifted her eyes to his face.

Spence's first inclination was to smirk at the irony of the situation, but recalling their last encounter, suddenly there was not much about it that was all that funny. "She was reading to me from the Bible," he admitted.

"Oh." She offered no further comment.

"That's all right. We can just talk."

"No," she answered almost defensively. "I know how to read. Where is it, your Bible?"

Spence sighed as he indicated the table at his bedside. He could sense her graceful movements as she stepped around and picked up the book.

"Okay, where do you want me to start?" she asked as he heard her flipping through the filmy pages.

A sudden thought came to him. "Um, the Gospel of John." He swallowed as a lump rose in his throat. *Lord, help me.* "Chapter. . .eight."

"John. . .John. . .where is it?"

"There's a table of contents at the beginning with page numbers." An uncomfortable heat began to rise into his face. Maybe this was not the time or place or the proper way to do this. But who knew if there would ever be another one?

"Okay, here it is," she said cheerfully.

Too late. . . .

"Chapter eight, you said?" She continued leafing through the text. "This is kind of long. Do you want me to read the whole thing?"

"Just start at the beginning," he answered in a quiet voice. He knew she would stop at the appropriate place.

"Okay. Here we go. 'Jesus returned to the Mount of Olives, but early the next morning he was back again at the Temple. A crowd soon gathered, and he sat down and talked to them. As he was speaking, the Jewish leaders and Pharisees brought a woman caught in adultery and placed her out in front of the staring crowd.' "

Spence unconsciously held his breath while Lori's voice faltered.

Slowly she started again, " ' "Teacher," they said to Jesus, "this woman was caught in the very act of adultery. Moses' law says to kill her. What about it?" '

" 'They were trying to trap him into saying something they could use against him, but Jesus stooped down and wrote in the dust with his finger. They kept demanding an answer, so he stood up again and said, "All right, hurl the stones at her until she dies. But only he who never sinned may throw the first!" '

" 'Then he stooped down again and wrote some more in the

dust. And the Jewish leaders slipped away one by one, beginning with the eldest, until only Jesus was left in front of the crowd with the woman.'

" 'Then Jesus stood up again and said to her, "Where are your accusers? Didn't even one of them condemn you?" '

" ' "No, sir," she said.' "

Lori's voice had grown weaker and weaker until she stopped reading altogether.

"'And Jesus said,'" Spence continued, his voice hoarse with emotion, "'"Neither do I. Go and sin no more." ' "

Neither of them spoke for a time. Spence lifted another petition heavenward, hoping he had done the right thing. "Lori?" he whispered.

"What?" Her voice was barely audible.

"Will you talk to me?"

He heard her let loose a shuddering sigh before she finally spoke. "Okay, so I'm a tainted woman. Like that's any big news."

"Hey, come on. Let me in."

"Why?" Her tone was no longer weak. It held an edge of anger and iciness.

"Because," Spence replied, fortifying his own emotions as well, "I care about you."

There was a brief silence, as if she were stunned. "Humph!" she scoffed. "I doubt it. If you really knew me—"

"But I do. Far better than I think you know yourself."

"I know *exactly* who I am!" she whispered forcefully. "I am everything my father ever said I was. You know, he got my mother pregnant before they were married. He called her a whore. And after that nigh—" She broke off. "He said I was just like her. . .and so I am."

"Lori, you're not a whore."

"Give me a break. You haven't the least idea of the things I've done."

Spence shook his head. "I don't want to know."

"Why not?" she challenged. "You afraid of how bad I might be?"

"No. I don't think you could tell me anything that would surprise me. Or anything that matters."

"Oh, yeah. Well how about a story of a basically content, fifteen-year-old girl. Has everything money can buy. Lots of friends, big house, her own room, no siblings. Anything she wants. Then one day, she finds out that none of this stuff is free. It never has been. There's been a hidden price all along. Just like everything else."

"Lori," he interrupted. He tried to hide his clenched fist beneath the sheets as a tightness cinched his gut. "If you don't want to tell me this, you—"

"Oh, come now, Spence," she continued recklessly, "isn't this what you wanted to know? 'Let me in,' you always say. Okay! Like I said, there was a price. And that price was me. Everything I thought was mine, wasn't. It was his. . .everything."

Anger surged deep within Spence. It mingled with a feeling of nausea and disbelief. "Your father?"

"His political colleagues. It seems I was a convenient form of recreation for his running mate's son." There were several seconds of silence. "Anyway," she resumed, "I don't think of him as my father. I don't think of him at all."

"Don't lie to me. I know you still think about him. I know you still have contact with him."

"Not anymore! I'm leaving."

"Leaving?" Spence felt a wave of panic wash over him. "Where?"

"Oh, I mean. . .just him. I've decided I'm through with his games."

"That's why you moved in with Maggie?"

"Yes."

Another realization. "Did that break-in have anything to do with—"

"Yes."

"Lori," he urged her, "you realize you're not going to be safe anywhere you might run. You've got to stop this guy. All of them. Get them behind bars."

She laughed bitterly. "You don't know Donald Jacobs. He could talk his way out of a Spanish inquisition."

"I think you're overestimating his power."

"I'm not," she argued. "He can get away with things that . . .I don't know. He just can."

"Lori, don't you see? You're still seeing him through the eyes of an awestruck, fearful young girl. Outside, you grew up. Inside. . .you didn't."

"So what? Are you saying I'm immature?" With each question she grew angrier.

"No, I'm saying you have to face up to what he did. How he copped out as a father. He was supposed to be there to protect you, shield you. Your choices made as an adult were directly affected by him. And most importantly, none of it is your fault."

Silence answered him.

"Lorelei Sommers, you've been trying your whole life to live up to something you thought your daddy might eventually love. There is no love in people like him."

"So," she finally shot back, "I suppose now you want me to accept the love of your God? This wonderful Father? Let Him be the father to me that I never had, right?"

"Well, yes." He was slightly taken aback by her direct line of questioning. It seemed she had heard something of God before. . .although he was not sure he wanted to know just how or what she had learned.

"No thanks! I've had my fill of 'fathers' for this lifetime. That's why I'm leaving altogether. But perhaps you'd like a crack at me next? Show me how saintly you can be, so you might 'win me honest'?"

Spence winced at her words, recognizing them for what they were. . .extreme and deep pain. Nonetheless, they hurt. "I don't think I deserved that," he muttered through clenched teeth.

He heard her shuffling her feet on the tiled floor. "You're right. I'm sorry, Spence. But I need you to know that I can't let myself need anyone. For the first time in my life, I've figured out how to do things on my own."

Spence nodded glumly. It was no use trying to interject how no one can live without God. She was just too faraway to even comprehend such a thought. "Doesn't it matter that I care about you?" he asked miserably.

"I don't know what it's like to be cared about without any strings attached," she said hoarsely as she grasped his hands. "And I don't want to find out." Even the tiny shocks of electricity he felt at her touch did little to alleviate the cold numbness that pervaded his soul.

"And I can't return something I don't understand," she continued. "You need. . .no, you *deserve* someone who can. Someone good."

"Lori," he argued. But she quickly put a finger to his lips.

"Shh. I'm going to go now."

He clutched desperately at her hand. "Please. . .come and see me again."

"As a friend?"

"As anything you're willing to be. My patches come off Friday. We'll find out then if the surgery worked." He squeezed her hands tightly. "It would mean a lot to me if you were here."

"I'll try."

He let her hands go as she began to pull away from his side.

"Goodbye, Spence."

He was determined not to say goodbye. Not yet. "Break a leg tonight."

She did not answer, but he heard her moving across the room and then the sound of the door clicking shut. His eyes began to burn and itch beneath the gauze.

Flopping dejectedly back against his pillow, he raised his face upward. "I hope You can mend broken hearts."

fifteen

"Are you ready to get started, Spence?" Dr. Bray asked.

"Yeah, in a minute." He turned to Corinne who had been at his side. "Is she here yet?" he whispered in her direction.

"Sorry, Spence." She squeezed his hand in a sympathetic gesture.

He nodded solemnly, relieved that Corinne was the only one he had told about Lori's expected appearance. It was obvious she was not coming, and the one thing he did not need was everyone's pity.

"All righty. Let's peel these babies off, Doc." Spence gave a slight grin.

A hush fell over the room as Dr. Bray began to unwind the layers of gauze, then smoothly peel off the surgical tape that held the patches over Spence's eyes. Spence tried not to laugh at how quiet everyone had suddenly become, as if no one was breathing.

"Now, when I get the first one off, keep your eye shut. I want you to open them both, slowly, at the same time."

Spence nodded.

"Would somebody dim the lights, please?" Dr. Bray asked.

Finally, the last piece of covering was carefully lifted from Spence's face. The air felt strange on his skin after being covered for even those few days.

"Okay, Spence. Just open them real slow."

He consciously moved the muscles near his eyelids, finding he had to concentrate on the usually involuntary movement. Some matter had apparently helped fuse them together. Slowly, the lids parted, and he blinked. He was aware of light. At first he thought this nothing too exciting. . .until he remembered that the lights had been dimmed. With hope gathering in his heart, Spence blinked several more times.

Spence noticed his hand, lying in his lap. . .he *saw* it. His pulse raced as he wiggled his fingers for the sheer joy of just watching them move. Then, he lifted his eyes. There, all about him, blurry, yet distinguishable, were the faces of all those he loved. A lump grew in his throat, and he was afraid tears might come and blur his new-found vision even more.

It dawned on him that everyone was waiting for his response. With a grin that nearly hurt his cheeks in its width, he focused on his mother at the foot of his bed. "Hi, Mom. . .you cut your hair."

Anyone walking down the halls of St. Luke's could not have avoided hearing the whoops, whistles, and laughter coming from Room 209.

❧

Lori slumped against the coolness of the park bench. Tilting her head back, she closed her eyes and tried to block out thoughts of the last several days. *If only I could erase the last several years.* A finch's song in a nearby tree caught her ear, and she glanced up. For a brief moment his song uplifted her heavy heart. She looked over the small lake. The sun was beginning its descent behind the trees, and the early evening's calm wind was gently lapping the waves along the rocky shore.

Several couples passed in front of her on the worn path, oblivious to all else around them. The memory of the evening she had spent at the lake with Spence, painful in its sweetness, flooded her heart. Why, oh, why couldn't she have a normal life like everyone else?

With a weary, resigned sigh, she glanced at her watch. She should be getting on to the theater soon to prepare for the evening's performance. *Friday.* . . . She knew where she should be, but that was one place she could not go. She honestly hoped Spence would quickly get over any disappointment he might feel. But the mere thought of having to start all over with him bothered her. For one time in her life, she had not had to depend on her beauty, and she had liked it. Hard as it was to admit, she had even begun to get used to it.

Spence may have been a lot of things, but he was still a person, just like everyone else. And since her looks were the deciding factor with the others. . .well, they would be with him, too. She knew. It was only a matter of time.

Releasing any further thoughts of him, she stood up and headed toward the theater. She still had plenty of time, and she wanted to make the most of it. Unbeknownst to anyone else, her suitcase lay packed and waiting in the Penny Lane costume room. After tomorrow night's finale, it was ready to be picked up and hauled onto the 11:30 P.M. flight to Denver. What she would do after that she did not know. She had a bit of cash to make it for a few days. There had to be a theater there somewhere. . .she hoped.

As Lori neared the vicinity of Penny Lane, she saw a group of people standing in a small cluster near a café. They stood quite still for a time before finally splitting up and heading in various directions down and across the street.

Not really giving them a second thought, she continued down the walk. A friendly voice caught her attention. "Lovely evening, tonight."

She stopped and turned to see a tall, attractive young woman smiling at her. Lori did not respond.

"Would you happen to have a moment?"

"Why? Are you selling something?" What was she doing? She always bypassed these clowns in the street.

"No. Really, I'd just like to give you something." She rather shyly handed Lori a small pamphlet. "Read it if you get a chance."

Lori glanced at the paper and did a double take. She did not know whether to laugh or cry. *Does Life Seem Empty to You? There Is a Solution.* She flipped it open. All the same Bible verses were there. In an instant she was eight years old again, standing next to her grandfather on a street corner in downtown Nashville.

"Grandpa, why do you do this?"

"Because, Lori, God loves every single person He created. And I love God. I want to help others to see. . .to feel that love."

It had seemed like such a simple answer back then. But her grandfather was not a simple man. So what was it? Was there more? Lori tried in vain to recall anything else from her summers spent with her grandparents on their ranch. But that was part of the problem—only the summers.

By the time she had returned back home, life continued in its usual fashion. Sunday was the one day off from public appearances, with the exception of the occasional publicity shot of the little family attending services.

It was all so cloudy now. It had been too long since she had heard those words from her grandparents firsthand. And it seemed even longer since she had thought of them as applying to her.

"Thanks," she finally acknowledged the brunette woman before her. "But I'm really not. . . . I don't need this."

She pressed it back into the woman's hand and started to walk away.

"Wait!"

Lori turned back around to find the woman running after her. "If you won't take it, could I at least. . .pray with you?" She fidgeted nervously.

Lori smiled kindly at her. She was really trying. "Look. I know exactly how you feel here, although I must admit it's been quite a few years." The woman's eyes widened in surprise. "But there is one thing I guess you haven't learned yet. All those verses. . .those promises. . . ." She nearly choked with emotion on the last word. Swallowing hard, she regained control. "They're only for a select few. My grandparents are two of them. And. . .one other person I know. I used to think maybe. . .at one time. Things happen. . . ." She shook her head, turned, and left the young woman to try and piece together the encounter.

The remainder of the walk to the theater was spent deep in thought. How she would get the understudy to take her role immediately. And how she might get that flight to Denver tonight. It had been far too long already.

❧

Spence pushed up the wire-framed aviator glasses. He could not help the gleeful expression he was sure permeated every movement as he trounced around his old stomping grounds, this time taking everything in through his eyes. He had forgotten how gorgeous the Penny Lane Theater was.

"Hey, Spence," Mike called over to him. "Show's about to start. You wanna sit up in the booth with me?"

"Thanks for the invite, buddy. But I want to be in my place in the pit."

Mike shrugged and nodded in understanding. Just then, Diane, the young woman from Spence's church, who now had a face to go with her name, bounced up to Mike and whispered something in his ear. He laughed heartily and leaned over to place a solid kiss on her lips before she scurried off toward backstage.

"I guess you miss more than obvious things when you can't see, eh?" Spence sent a teasing smile to his friend, who, completely out of character, flushed slightly.

"Yeah, Diane's a nice woman. I've even been going to church with her once in awhile. Between what she's explaining to me and what you've said before, things are sort of starting to make sense."

Spence walked briskly over to his friend and clapped him soundly on the back before giving him a quick embrace. "I'm glad," he said. And he meant it. "Didn't really figure her to be your type, though," he jested.

"Yeah, well. . .things change. I never thought Lori to be

exactly your type, either."

Spence lowered his eyes as he felt some of the life drain out of him.

"Hey, I'm sorry," Mike said as he clasped a hand on Spence's shoulder. "That was a dumb thing to say."

Spence took a deep breath before lifting his head. "Forget it."

"I better get up to my post." Mike gave Spence's shoulder one last pat before taking the steps to the sound booth two, at a time.

Spence weaved his way down to the orchestra pit until he found his familiar spot at the piano. For a moment, he even closed his eyes and just listened to the hum of the crowded auditorium. The feeling of anticipation that hung in the air was nearly thick enough to reach out and touch.

"Spence!" Bob hissed from the wings. He motioned for him to meet him backstage.

Spence glanced nervously at his watch as he stepped through the side door. "What is it?" he asked when he saw the stage manager's worried face.

"I just wanted you to be prepared. It's Lori. She hasn't shown yet. Christine is her understudy and is ready to step in but—"

"What do you mean she's not here?" He tried to control the panic from creeping into his tone.

Bob shrugged. "Apparently she mentioned something to Christine about having to catch a plane last night and—"

The orchestra's pre-performance tuning was starting. Spence closed his eyes and rubbed his temples wearily. "I've gotta get back to the pit. Tell Christine. . .she'll do fine."

❧

Spence's eyes fluttered open when the house lights began to dim, and he focused his attention on the stage. He tried to get into the spirit of the musical, but it was hard to work around the ache in his chest. It even seemed to affect his playing, and he hoped the notes sounded better to everyone else than they did to him.

The opening began with Todd and Cole, and Spence began to wish things would hurry along. Despite the fact that he wanted to savor this last production at Penny Lane, each note, each line was now a thing to be endured. How could she have just left?

He mechanically followed the script into the second scene of the sleepy Scottish village, partially misted over in the glen with the help of fog machines. The time came for Christine's appearance.

When she first waltzed onto the stage, Spence had to look down. After the endless hours of rehearsals, Lori had firmly established herself in his mind. Everything about her just fit. And now, to watch someone else. . . .

Finally chiding himself for being unprofessional, he glanced up.

What he saw made him look down again before returning his gaze to the stage. *Lori.* His eyes began to mist, and he rubbed them stubbornly so he would not miss one second. Shining blond hair hung gracefully down her shoulders with the side portions done up in a braided coronet that encircled her head in golden glory. Even from this distance, he could see the lightness of her eyes and longed to be nearer so he might study their clear green depths.

He watched in fascination as she became the character of Fiona Campbell. Her speech, her movements, everything. . .and always her voice. She was completely separated from all else. And the notes hung in the air like just discovered dreams. This beautiful young woman was truly blessed with a gift for the theater.

As the scenes and acts progressed, Spence realized he was surprised at the lack of awe he had experienced over her fragile beauty. True, she was a glorious vision to behold, and his first sight of her had almost stopped his breath, especially since he had come so close to not seeing her at all.

But he had had a glimpse of her that no one else had. And he silently thanked God for that one blessing of his blindness. There had been no pretense in their relationship. Lori had been real with him.

Too soon the curtain fell, and he found himself standing with the rest of the zealous audience, applauding his heart out.

Lori was presented with her bouquet of roses, and he thought he saw a hint of tears in her eyes as she cradled them in her arms. He found his own throat tightening as well. He knew that if she had not left last night, tonight was a sure thing. This would be it.

Just then, a running flash caught Spence's eye and he looked up, astonished to find Mike on stage with a hand-held microphone.

"Ladies and gentlemen," Mike began, "may I have your attention, please." He waited for the murmurs to soften. "If you've ever attended any other Penny Lane performances, the name Spencer Berg won't be unfamiliar to you."

What was he doing?

"This musical was certainly no exception, enjoying its direction under his hand. Although he was not aware we were going to do this, we'd like to share a few things that have happened in his life lately."

Spence rolled his eyes as he shook his head with a smile. He flopped back down onto the piano bench, meeting the grins of the entire orchestra.

"First of all," Mike continued, "just yesterday, after over a year of blindness resulting from an accident, Spence regained his eyesight due to a wonderful new surgery."

The crowd exploded into applause, and Spence felt his very soul lift in joy.

"Secondly, this is a bit of melancholy news for us, but Spence has been offered a writing contract with a major music company in Nashville."

Again, the crowd erupted into clapping and whistles. "We're proud to send him down there, but at the same time, saddened to see him go. Spence," Mike motioned to him with his hand, "will you come up here, please?"

Spence started to shake his head but several prodding hands in the orchestra quickly got him moving up the stage steps. He stepped toward Mike, still shaking his head in disbelief mingled with embarrassment.

"We thought it might be appropriate to have Spence sing one or two of his songs for us. What do you think?" Mike asked the huge audience. Their answer was an immediate round of cheers and more long whistles. "That's what I thought," Mike said with a grin. "It's all yours, buddy."

After his friend had replaced the microphone in its stand, Spence turned around at the sound of wheels being rolled across the hardwood floor and was greeted by one of the baby grands. He smiled at the two actors who had pushed it on stage before he sat down at the bench and adjusted the mike.

He took a moment to fight the bright lights and scan the varied faces in the crowd. "It's really good to see you again," he quipped and was rewarded with their light laughter.

Taking a deep breath, Spence leveled his gaze toward the wings just in time to see a blond head dip behind a curtain. This would be his last chance. With a sigh, he started the soft intro he had worked at for so long.

"This is one of the songs that helped get me my contract," he said quietly. "It would never have been completed without a certain person to inspire me to finish it. This song will always belong to her."

His fingers eased out a slow vamp for a few measures before he closed his eyes and tilted his head toward the mike:

> "The look that says so many things
> with nary a spoken word.
> Glances flash amid whispered dreams,
> thoughts that needn't be heard,

eyes drowning with emotion.
We can't quite get past the tears
to grasp the courage to profess a love
we know would last the years.

"Can't we try just one more time?
Take my hand and you will see
there are oh, so many reasons
you should belong to me.
Please, let's try it one last time.
Apart our souls will bleed.
We know that in each other's arms
together's all we need.

"I know you have some sadness,
I realize your pain.
But you see, I can help heal your wounds
our hearts are much the same.
I'm ready and I'm willing
to go where this might lead.
I only want to be with you
You're all I'll ever need.

"Can't we try just one more time?
Take my hand and you will see
there are oh, so many reasons
you should belong to me.
Please, let's try it one last time.
Apart our souls will bleed.
We know that in each other's arms
together's all we need."

Spence gently lifted his fingers from the keys, his eyelids still closed. *Oh, Lord, let her have heard it this time.*

❧

Lori clung to the seam of the heavy velvet curtain as the audience broke into reverent applause. Her knees felt quite weak, and she was not sure if she remembered how to breathe.

Disjointed thoughts flitted about her brain. . .her father's threats, the phone call with her grandmother, that silly sign hanging in front of Spence's church about abundant life, bits and pieces of the passage out of the Bible she had read aloud in the hospital, but most of all, Spence, himself.

Swirling in and out of her consciousness, they just did not piece together. . .they made no sense. And worse yet, they left her feeling completely out of control.

Every time she shook her head to clear the fog, all that appeared was Spence's honest face. . .his impish grin. . .and those penetrating brown eyes.

She raised her eyes to the stage and slowly tuned in as she realized Spence was about to sing again, just catching the last of his words.

"As Mike explained, the Lord has been doing some great things in my life. And nothing gives me more pleasure than to know I'll be writing music for Him. It hardly seems an adequate thanks for all He's done, but I know He understands. His grace truly is amazing."

He grasped the microphone from the stand and strolled to the center of the stage. Apparently he was going to do this one a cappella.

"Amazing grace, how sweet the sound," his strong tenor effortlessly coaxed out the words and melody of "Amazing Grace," a popular folk hymn written by John Newton.

> "That saved a wretch like me.
> I once was lost, but now am found,
> was blind, but now I see."

Lori blinked back the hot tears that were starting to form.

" 'Twas grace that taught my heart to fear,
and grace my fears relieved;
How precious did that grace appear
the hour I first believed."

The words cut her like a knife, and she slipped down to the floor, oblivious to anyone or anything around her. It was as though a light had been flipped on, making a dismal room strangely bright.

All of her past, all of her hurts, every pain and fear she had ever known, fled from that light. A tremendous heaviness simply vanished, and Lori nearly turned around to see if anyone had physically lifted something off her.

"Through many dangers, toils, and snares,
I have already come.
'Tis grace has brought me safe thus far,
and grace will lead me home."

Hunched over her knees, Lori let the quiet sobs escape. "I'm so sorry, God. I'm just so sorry." She did not know what else to say. She only knew she had to say something to alleviate the sweet ache inside her.

"When we've been there ten thousand years,
bright shining as the sun.
We've no less days to sing God's praise,
than when we first begun."

Lori slowly lifted her heaving chest to see the curtain falling in front of Spence. He stood with his shoulders hunched, his back to the wings.

She desperately wanted to run to him, to tell him that she could stay. To tell him that she finally understood his love.

But she didn't. It was simply too much to fathom all at one time.

"I'm sorry, Spence," she whispered.

Before he could turn in her direction, she slipped down the backstage stairs and trotted to the dressing room. It did not take long to throw off her costume and put on her jeans and blouse.

Taking a last few swipes at her face with cold cream, she grabbed up her small suitcase and her duffel bag and glanced around the room for the last time. "Good-bye, ol' Penny Lane. I could've grown used to you."

Just as quickly, she shook off her emotions. She had a plane to catch. She glanced at her watch and headed for the door. At the last minute, she turned back and strode over to the costume rack. Pulling off one curly brown wig and a subtly colored sack dress, she stuffed them in her duffel bag and strode through the door without a second glance. She would return them later.

❧

Spence smiled half-heartedly at all the well-wishers in the wings as he tried to snake his way through the throng of people. Every so often he'd raise up on his tiptoes in search of a blond head.

"Spence!"

He whirled around at Mike's voice.

"Spence!" He waved over the crowd of actors and barreled his way through them. "She heard it."

A smile started across his face. "Where? Where is she?"

Mike's face sobered. "Nobody can find her."

Someone might as well have punched Spence in the gut. He stared at the floor, the spot where she had been standing only minutes ago. "She's gone."

"You don't know that. Maybe she just—"

Spence shook his head. "She's gone. It wasn't enough."

sixteen

Lori sprinted through the terminal straight for gate seven. She breathed a sigh of relief when she heard the final boarding call for flight 609 to Denver. She was not too late.

Hurriedly showing her ticket to the stewardess, she squeezed her way down the narrow aisle of the 727 until she found her seat. It did not look like a completely booked flight, so she helped herself to the window seat.

Flopping down, she pushed up the small shade covering the window and stared out at the runway lights and past them to the lights of Minneapolis. For the first time in her life, she regretted leaving someplace. Or was it someone?

The announcement over the airplane's PA system broke her reverie as the stewardess instructed all passengers to take their seats and fasten their safety belts. Lori buckled hers dutifully and tuned out the rest of the speech she had heard a hundred times, concentrating instead on the view outside.

She let her fingertips lightly touch the pane as she stubbornly fought against her just-as-determined tears. "Goodbye, Spencer," she said quietly.

At that moment a passenger settled into the seat next to her. She quickly cleared her throat and wiped her fingers across her cheeks to erase any telltale tears. She earnestly hoped the person did not expect her to make small talk all the way to Chicago for their layover.

As she continued her perusal of the airfield, she remembered the abundance of empty seats on this flight and was suddenly annoyed. Why couldn't the newcomer have picked any one of them? Some people had absolutely no manners whatsoever. Oh, well. She would just feign a trip to the restroom and take a seat farther back, that's all. There were still a few minutes until takeoff.

She turned around to be excused and met with the coldest pair of blue eyes. Her breath stuck in her throat, and she felt herself growing dizzy. Closing her eyes, she shook her head, hoping, praying he was not there.

"Good evening, Lori."

She felt like crying. Why? Why, when she had been so close?

"Very touching little farewell there."

She opened her eyes and forced herself to meet his stare.

"Do you think he'll miss you much?"

"You leave Spence out of this," she hissed. And as an afterthought, "And you leave him alone."

He chuckled. "Oh, relax, little lady. He's clean."

She narrowed her eyes as her courage began to grow. "You'd better not lay a hand on him or—"

"My, but we're possessive, aren't we?" He smiled sardonically and ran a hand through his perfectly groomed sandy hair. "John might be jealous." He closed his eyes and laid his head against the backrest.

"Can't you just leave me alone?" she seethed.

He turned his head toward her and opened one eye. "You know, I'd really like to, love. Do you think I enjoy playing baby sitter? Jaunting all over the place keeping tabs on a spoiled little princess?"

"I haven't done anything," she declared.

Several people turned to look back at her. She gulped and vowed to remember to keep her voice low.

"Not yet, anyway," he agreed. "And you certainly won't now."

Lori huffed and slammed her back against the chair. "So, where is it now? From Chicago to—"

"Tallahassee," he finished for her. "Apparently your father thinks you may be homesick."

She gave him a sidelong glare. "Don't you ever get sick of

being their lackey? Their slick-looking, trained monkey in a business suit—"

His hand shot out and grabbed her arm in a tight grip. "Watch it," he muttered through clenched teeth. "I already told you this isn't my first choice for climbing the political ladder. But I'll do what I have to do. And be warned," he said, leaning his face uncomfortably close to hers, "I'll take whatever's in my way and do with it what I please." His lips curled in a wicked smile.

Lori jerked her arm free and slunk as close to the window as she could. She watched as he closed his eyes again and then she looked helplessly out the window as the plane began to taxi down the runway.

She remembered the words to Spence's song and to the hymn that followed. Then she closed her eyes and did the only thing she had left to do—something she had not done since she had been a very little girl.

Dear God, I need your help. I know I don't deserve it but. . .I just can't go back there.

It certainly did not seem like much of a prayer to her, but it had been a long time. She just hoped that after all these years, He was still listening.

❧

"We will be landing at O'Hare International Airport in a few minutes," the voice on the loudspeaker intoned. "Please fasten your seat belts, and stay seated until the plane has come to a complete stop. Thank you for flying Midwestern Airlines."

Lori watched as the jet circled above brilliantly lit Chicago, then glanced over at her "companion." She did not even know his name. She had not known any of their names. But they were all the same. . .the ever-present eyes, watching where her father could not be.

It would not be long now. They would disembark and likely hop onto a private Lear jet, already waiting their arrival. She glanced down at the huge airport, searching in vain for the vehicle that would mean the end of her freedom. Inwardly, she laughed scornfully. As if she had ever been free.

Too soon, they rolled to a stop and passengers began collecting their gear and heading toward the exit. Lori waited until he had stepped into the aisle, then reached overhead for her duffel bag.

He took it from her and tucked it under his arm. "Allow me," he asserted and offered his other arm for her to take.

Lori eyed him suspiciously then tore the duffel bag loose from his grasp. "Thanks," she muttered as she pushed past, "I can carry my own luggage."

He dogged her every step into the terminal until they finally reached a grouping of chairs. She flopped down on one of them, staring at him as he stood over her.

He stretched out his hand toward her. "Let's move. There are people waiting on us."

Refusing his hand, she stood with a sigh, hefted her duffel bag over her shoulder, and followed him down the corridor. *Anytime now, God.*

She trudged after him several more minutes, trying to forget who she was and where she was headed. Perhaps concentrating on the people around her would help her to forget. . . momentarily.

She had to smile when she saw a young family ambling along in front of them. The father was holding his pregnant wife's hand while their enthusiastic toddler intermittently darted several feet ahead and back again. Their obviously happy faces reminded her of Spence's family. How she longed to know what that kind of happiness felt like.

"I'm going to get a cup of coffee."

She looked back to her guardian's face as he nodded toward a small snack bar. She dumped her belongings onto a nearby bench and sat down to wait for him. The thought of taking off and running was ludicrous. He would surely catch up with her, and where would she run to, anyway?

She saw him glancing her way several times as he ordered his coffee. Letting out a long breath, she reached over and picked up a magazine someone had left. Flipping distractedly through the pages, she noticed the sign for the women's restroom several yards ahead of her. It was then that the thought came to her. She did not know from where. . .or how. . .but it came.

She fidgeted nervously with the periodical as he returned with his steaming beverage. "Okay, let's go."

She steeled her courage as she stood up. "I. . .I have to use the restroom."

He whirled around and studied her carefully.

She tried to look as natural as possible. "What are you looking at? I said I have to use the ladies' room."

He looked from the restroom door back to her several times, considering the situation. He took a sip of coffee and nodded. "All right. But hurry up. We've got another plane to catch."

She nodded, honestly grateful, and headed toward the door at a steady clip.

Once inside she found an empty stall, locked it behind herself, and leaned against it wearily. *Pull yourself together, Lori. You've gotta get out of here. Fast!*

Hurrying out of her jeans and shirt, she shimmied into the huge sack dress and began tying her hair up and back. She pulled the curly mop of a wig out of the bag and fluffed it up a bit before placing it on her head.

Digging through the remainder of the contents, she was relieved to find a pair of sandals stuffed in the bottom. She had almost forgotten about replacing her tennis shoes.

Hoping she looked adequately different, she stepped from the stall and over to the large trash can. She rummaged through her purse for her few important items, then stuffed it and the duffel bag under several heaps of discarded paper towels in the gray metal container.

Now, a step over to the mirror above the sink. It might work, but. . . . She leaned over and looked at her face. She still looked too much like herself. Fear began to cinch her heart as she realized time was getting away from her. This was not going to work.

A soft, muffled crying reached her ears from the opposite end of the room and she momentarily forgot about her predicament. Searching out the source, she walked down the long line of stalls, peering into each one. When she came to the last, she spied a tiny boy of no more than three, sobbing into a faded blue blanket.

She bent down next to him. "Are you lost?"

He lifted his tear-streaked face and his large brown eyes widened when he saw her. "Mommy?"

She then recognized him as the rambunctious child she had been studying earlier. He must have become separated from his family.

"No, honey. But I'll help you find your mommy. Okay?"

He nodded and stood to his feet, eagerly taking her hand. "You look like my mommy," he stated as he stared up at her.

Lori stopped in front of the mirror and did a double take. She did. The short curly brown hair, the sack dress. . . . That was it! "Thank You, God," she cried softly.

She kneeled down in front of the little boy once more. "My name is Lori. What's your name?" she asked him kindly.

"Danny."

"Okay, Danny." She smiled. "I'm going to help you find your mom and dad. But I want you to do one thing for me."

"What?" His weepy brown eyes were curious.

"I want to borrow your blanket."

He clutched it possessively.

"I'll give it back. Just as soon as we find your mommy. I promise. I just want to. . .hold it for you. To make sure it doesn't get lost. Okay?"

He glanced at it one last time and reluctantly handed it over. Lori promptly stuffed it underneath her dress in a gently rounded fashion. His eyes grew wider still.

"Now you really look like Mommy."

Lori grinned at him. She took a damp paper towel to wipe his face and proceeded to take his hand. "Okay, Danny. Let's go."

Stopping at the door, she took a deep breath. *It's now or never, God. Here we go.*

Lori strode purposefully into the corridor, not so much as sneaking a peek toward the grouping of seats where she knew her guard waited. She started toward the upcoming gates, in search of the youngster's folks. She knew she still did not have much time. And if *he* happened to spy her standing next to the child's mother. . . .

"There's Daddy," the boy piped up. He dropped Lori's hand and ran headlong into his father's waiting arms. The parent's face immediately showed such intense relief that Lori almost forgot she was a participant in the whole affair.

But when Danny's father opened his eyes, he, too, looked at her in shock. "Did you. . . ?"

She strode over to them. "I found him in the bathroom."

"Thank you! Thank you so much!" He did not try to hide the tears welling up in his eyes.

"You're most welcome." She smiled, cherishing the feeling of her good deed.

Danny was suddenly tugging on her hand, leading toward the jet way that snaked out to the awaiting plane. "Lori, come and meet my mommy. See how she looks like you."

Danny's father laughed as he took her other arm. "Yes, you must meet my wife. You do bear an incredible resemblance to her. She's waiting down by the plane. She thought maybe Danny would show up there. I was busy trying to look everywhere else."

The reunion of Danny and his mother was just as joyous as the one between him and his father. The nearly frantic woman wept as she scooped the curly headed boy into her arms and smothered his face with kisses. "Oh, thank God! Thank God you're all right."

When she looked up, she, too, did not hide her look of surprise at seeing Lori.

"I can't thank you enough," she reiterated for the hundredth time. "It's nice to know there are still people in the world you can trust."

Lori just smiled. "Oh, Danny. I almost forgot." She reached down the neck of her oversized dress and unceremoniously pulled out the crumpled piece of blue flannel. Even she had to laugh at their expressions. "It's a long story," she explained.

The last boarding call was announced, and Danny and his parents reluctantly moved toward the door. "Lori," his father stated. "Is there something. . .anything we can do for you?"

"Well," she smiled weakly, "thank you, but I really don't think so."

"Please, anything," his wife insisted.

"You wouldn't happen to have an extra ticket, would you?" she teased.

The two glanced at each other, astounded. "Are you serious? Is that what you need?"

Lori nodded, wondering what was going on.

"We got bumped off our last flight because they overbooked," the woman explained. "So they gave us a voucher for a free, one-way ticket to the destination of our choice. We don't have much use for it." She dug in her purse for it. "Please, we'd love for you to have it."

Lori reached out with a shaky hand and accepted her ticket to freedom. "Now I know there is a God," she stated boldly. She leaned over and ruffled Danny's hair. "Tell me, little man. Where is this plane going?"

"Home." He beamed. "Home to Tennessee."

seventeen

Lori pushed the curry brush over and over the sleek chestnut coat of her grandfather's prize mount, Flash. "That a boy," she murmured softly. "Feels nice, doesn't it?"

She smiled as the friendly horse leaned into the strokes. From the wall behind her, a portable radio tuned to the local Christian radio station was playing a medley of Christmas carols. Lori hummed along with "O Little Town of Bethlehem," feeling once again the new warmth that coursed through her.

This was her first Christmas where she finally understood what Christmas was truly all about. And that in itself made the whole holiday seem new. It had taken some time for her to begin to fathom God's love. But with her grandparents' help and her daily study of God's Word, she was learning.

"You're listening to WLOR out of Nashville," the announcer informed the audience. "Wishing you the merriest Christmas, the best kind. . .one full of God's love and peace."

Lori smiled as she continued her task of brushing down Flash.

"And now, straight from the Top Ten Christian Chart, we have the new number one song from Tyler Preston. A duet he's done with the industry's new mega-talent in song writing, Spencer Berg."

Lori's ears perked up at the mention of his name.

"We caught up with Tyler several days ago and were able to conduct a phone interview with him. Here's a brief sound bite."

"I'd love to take credit for 'Together's All We Need,' but that was Spence's baby. We have co-written several songs since then, though. He's really great to work with. A genuine talent."

"Tyler," the interviewer commented. "I'm sure you're aware

there are people out there who question the playing of this particular song on Christian radio stations. It's been said that the theme in regard to spiritual matters is, at the least, vague. Can you address that?"

"I'd love to, Kurt. One of The Way's goals is to reach a crossover audience. What that entails is not only writing songs and lyrics that have their base in a Christian perspective, but others that will get plenty of air time on secular stations.

"By getting our name and our music out there, we'll pull a larger, more diverse crowd into the music stores and into the concerts. Then, once they're there, the Gospel can be presented in a nonthreatening way. And since the artist is someone they're familiar with, they tend to be more open."

"Amen," Lori echoed. "They're not going to hear it in church if they're not there."

"So," the announcer was back, "here it is. The much-acclaimed song from the Preston and Berg duo, 'Together's All We Need.' "

The all-too-familiar intro wafted out of the speaker and Lori reached up to flick the switch off. It had been hard enough the first time she had heard it played on the air. It seemed no station she tuned into was a safe ground. . .they all carried it—often.

She felt genuinely happy for Spence's success, but the memories of the night he'd given the song to her were still too fresh, too painful.

Tears sprang up, and she wiped at them in irritation. It had been nearly six months now. When would it get easier?

"Lori?" her grandmother's voice called from the end of the stable.

"Comin', Gram." Lori hung the brush on its proper hook and lead the nickering gelding into his proper stall. "We'll go riding again tomorrow, I promise. Maybe by the river, eh?" She gave his muscled neck one last pat, thankful for the diversion he was to her healing heart, and strode toward the far door.

Her grandmother was standing just outside, holding their small, portable television, her eyes glued to the screen. "Come." She waved Lori forward with her hand. "Listen." She turned up the volume.

Lori gazed at the five-inch screen with interest. A perfectly coiffed anchor had just returned after a brief commercial. Her well-modulated voice coaxed out each word.

"And today in the political news arena, John Carlyle, son of Florida Governor Ted Carlyle, was indicted on several charges of rape and assault involving a number of underage girls."

A superimposed photo of John, Governor Carlyle, and Lori's father appeared in the upper corner of the screen.

"Also charged were Governor Carlyle himself and his Lieutenant Governor, Donald Jacobs, for offering hush money to the victims and their families in hopes that their political careers might continue on the road toward Washington."

The scene flashed to a video of the outside of the courthouse on the day of the pretrial hearing. Lori watched as several mobs of reporters scurried after the three men, shoving cameras and microphones in their blank, stony faces.

"Unconfirmed reports indicate that one of the first victims, and some say the one who blew the whistle on the cover-up, was Lieutenant Governor Jacobs's own daughter.

"John Carlyle faces three counts of rape and sexual assault, which in accordance with Florida law could earn him up to thirty years per charge. The other two men face lesser charges, but with the possibility of fifteen to twenty years in prison as well.

"On a happier note, in West Virginia today, some children are having a merrier Christmas than they'd ever thought possible. . . ."

Lori's grandmother turned the switch off and faced Lori. "I'm proud of you," she said softly. "You did the right thing."

Lori shrugged her shoulders. "I guess so. But it still hurts. Mom still won't talk to me."

"I know, sweetie. You'll have to give her time. And if she

still doesn't. . .well, it's in God's hands."

Lori smiled. "I love you, Gram." She reached over and gave the petite woman a warm hug.

"Come on," her grandmother urged. "We'll catch our death out in this cold. Besides, I have a Christmas surprise for you waiting in the house." Her eyes sparkled with mischief.

Lori sent her a questioning glance as she raced across the grounds to the sprawling ranch home. Snow gently blanketed the low roof, muting the multicolored Christmas lights that had just turned on in the growing dusk.

Once inside the front door, she kicked off her boots and shrugged out of her chore coat and gloves. Before she even placed them on the proper peg, a small but dense force tackled her legs, tiny arms wrapping themselves around her knees.

"Danny!" she cried as she scooped the little angel into her arms.

"Hi, Lori! I missed you!"

"Oh, I missed you, too!" She beamed and gave him another squeeze. "Did you bring your mom and dad?"

He nodded enthusiastically. "And my little sister."

"Great, let's go find 'em."

Phil and Marge Stevens met them halfway between the entry and the kitchen. They both greeted Lori warmly and wished her a Merry Christmas. But it was the baby in Marge's arms that held her attention.

At four months, little Ruth had filled out her once-scrawny newborn legs and her cheeks just begged to be chewed on. Her brown eyes twinkled merrily as she waved a chubby arm up and down.

"Could I?" Lori asked as she motioned toward the baby.

Marge promptly handed her over.

"I can't believe how big she's grown already." Lori shifted the little chunk to her other arm and clucked her tongue at her. It had seemed only a few weeks ago she had been born.

Lori recalled how the Stevenses had kept in contact with her since the flight to Tennessee, earnestly seeking her friendship in appreciation for all she had done in finding Danny.

When the time came for the Stevenses' baby to be born, Lori and her grandparents had been the recipients of one of their first phone calls and they promptly visited the hospital.

"She's a beautiful girl," Marge had said during that visit as she held out the sleeping bundle for Lori to hold. Exchanging a knowing glance with her husband, she continued. "We'd like to name her Lori. If you wouldn't mind."

Lori had looked up in shock. Someone wanted to name their baby after her? She looked down at the slumbering infant, so innocent and pure, naive to all the evils of the world. "Well," she hedged.

"Do you object?" Phil had asked.

"Oh, no. I mean, really, I'm more than honored. It's just that. . . . I guess I'm not too proud of some of the things I've done. I'd rather see her named after someone worthwhile."

"You know we love you, Lori," Marge had insisted. "But if you feel strongly about it, would you pick a name for her?"

Lori's eyes had widened at the awesome responsibility and privilege. Then she set her mind to thinking. "I've been reading about a lot of interesting people in the Bible lately. You know who sticks with me is Ruth. I mean, her husband died and she was left with basically nothing. She had the option of going home to her family or staying right where she was with things that were familiar, but she didn't.

"She chose to carry on with her mother-in-law, knowing that things wouldn't be easy, but also that that's where God wanted her to be." Lori had glanced down at the tiny face. "I've often wished that I had that courage."

"Ruth it is," Marge had declared.

"Ruth Margaret Stevens," Phil had then echoed.

And now here sat this growing little being, smiling with a disarming, toothless grin at Lori.

"We just wanted to stop in and wish you all a Merry Christmas on our way past. We're heading to Phil's folks in Kentucky, so we've a lengthy drive ahead of us." Marge smiled as she collected her squirming bundle from Lori's arms.

"Thank you for stopping. It wouldn't have been Christmas without seeing you." She reached over to the counter and plucked a candy cane from the decorated Mason jar, and handed it to Danny. "Now, don't give any to your sister," she reminded him with a smile.

"Oh, no." He shook his head adamantly. "She don't got no teeth."

They all laughed, and Lori helped them gather their things together as they walked to the door. "Take care," she called after them as they packed into their car and drove down the long, snow-covered drive.

She closed the door with a sigh.

"Say, darlin'," her grandfather interrupted her thoughts, "I need to do a bit of type shopping in Nashville. Care to come along?"

She turned toward the gray-headed man whose eyes twinkled with nearly as much impishness as little Danny's.

"All right, Grandpa. What's up your sleeve?"

"What a question to be asking at Christmas," he admonished with a grin. "You go get showered up and changed. We'll be leaving in a half-hour."

Lori shrugged and nodded her consent as she headed to her room. It was true. She needed to do some shopping of her own, and now was as good a time as any.

Once inside her bathroom, she shoved a tape into her boom box and went to turn on the water in the shower. When the sounds of soothing violin strings floated around the steamy air, her eyes again welled up with tears. As always. How long would it take to be able to listen to Purcell without thinking of him? It seemed everything somehow routed back to *him.*

She could not understand. She had been praying for months on end for God to take the pain, the loneliness away. But He hadn't. And in the meantime, Lori hobbled through her memories, testing the waters every so often and finding them still too deep.

She rose and flicked off the player. It was too soon.

❧

"Where are we going anyway?" Lori asked as she leaned over the front seat of her grandparents' car.

"Downtown," came her grandfather's response.

She sighed, knowing they were definitely up to something. She leaned back against the seat and studied the festive assortment of Christmas decorations that hung from the store fronts. She tried to keep her eyes open for any places that might hold gifts suitable for Grandpa and Gram. Her mind started to sift through a variety of possible presents when the car pulled into a parking spot.

She glanced out the window. A huge, four-storied building loomed over their car. "This doesn't look like a store, Grandpa." It was then that she leaned farther over and noticed the large sign above the door: THE WAY MUSIC CORPORATION.

Lori's stomach leaped into her throat as she stiffly sat back. She was aware of her grandparents' questioning looks. She winced at them imploringly and shook her head.

"Lori," her grandmother said firmly, yet with understanding. "It's time."

"Gram, I can't. I just—"

"Lorelei, the last thing you want to do is spend the rest of your life wondering, 'What if. . . ?' We'll be right here." She reached out and squeezed Lori's hand. "And God will be right there."

Lori glanced hopelessly out the window, knowing they were right. This should have been done a long time ago.

Taking a deep breath, she flipped open the door and stepped onto the curb. The building towered over her, making her feel infinitesimally small. *Come on, Lori. Chin up. This is no big deal. He may not even be there.* That last thought gave her the needed incentive to take the first step.

❧

Spence stared down at the paper before him, scribbled a few

notations with his pencil, and plunked out a few chords on the keyboard. *Just a few more lines.* He hummed the current melody he was working on as the words drifted through his mind.

Outside the window the sound of sleigh bells disrupted his concentration. His first inclination was to be perturbed, but he gave himself an inward shake. "Loosen up, Scrooge. After all, it is Christmas."

He shoved the papers away and stood abruptly, stretching his arms over his head as he wandered over to the large picture window. On the street below, a horse-drawn carriage clipped past at a brisk pace, its two passengers obviously enjoying the holiday mirth. He smiled, remembering the sleigh rides he and his family used to enjoy at a farm outside of Duluth. How many years ago that had been!

Spence leaned an arm against the glass and hummed a familiar holiday tune. Watching the fragile, fuzzy flakes of new snow float down past him, he again thanked God for the regained gift of his sight. He had forgotten how beautiful even the small things could be.

Two small boys were trying their mother's patience as she tried to hustle them into a car. They, on the other hand, were busy trying to catch snowflakes on their tongues.

Spence was reminded of all his favorite Christmas songs and activities. "Ah, thank You, Lord, for Christmas."

He gave one last smile at the scene before him.

"Spence?"

He glanced back to see Kim, one of the secretaries, standing in the door.

"Someone is here to see you."

He rolled his eyes. "Aw, Kim. I'm pretty much finished up here. I've gotta meet Tyler in twenty minutes and then rush home to meet my family." He began gathering his papers together and shoving them into his leather case.

"All right," she agreed. "I'll let her know. And have a Merry Christmas, Spence." She turned on her heel and walked back down the hall.

❧

Lori slipped into the back seat and shut the door. She met the expectant looks of her grandparents.

"He wasn't available."

They glanced at one another. "Maybe he'd already left," Gram suggested.

Lori nodded. "Maybe." She studied her purse for something to do. "I still need to do some shopping. You guys?"

She felt the car pull away from the curb, and she tried to ignore the dull ache in her heart.

❧

Lori slung the increasingly heavy shopping bag over her shoulder as she marched toward the center court in the mall. She was supposed to meet Gram and Grandpa there for a quick lunch, then go home again for further Christmas preparations. It was hard to believe Christmas was a mere two days away.

To her right, a throng of people, mostly younger children, hovered around the entrance of a music shop. Surprising herself, she directed her path toward the door. Jazzed up Christmas tunes were blaring through the store speakers in a cacophony of sound, nearly, but not quite, drowning out the excited chatter of the swarm.

Traipsing her way down the aisle toward the religious selections, Lori picked up the latest CD by Tyler Preston. The promo sticker heralded the inclusion of the smash hit 'Together's All We Need.' She flipped it over and studied the jacket photos, drawing in a breath when she saw a candid shot of Spence, leaning over piano keys, his eyes intense with concentration.

"Can I help you?" a friendly voice startled her.

"Oh—" She met the gaze of a store employee. "I didn't hear you."

"It's no wonder," he laughed as he nodded his head in the direction of the boisterous horde. "A signing party today. Tyler Preston."

"You're kidding! He's autographing his CDs?"

"Yep. You a fan?" He noted the disc she was still holding.

"Oh, me? Well, no. . .I mean yes, but. . . ."

"Nervous?" he chuckled.

She just shrugged her shoulders with a shy grin, not bothering to explain.

"Would you like me to have him sign it for you?"

Lori's eyes widened. "Oh, no. That's not really necessary—"

"Aw, no problem." He smiled charmingly and grasped the CD from her hand. "Working here I'll have a better chance of pushing through that crowd, anyway. What's your name?"

"Lori."

"I'll be right back."

Rolling her eyes in amusement mixed with embarrassment, she set back to the task of looking over the variety of artists. She honestly hoped that man would not think her some starstruck groupie after all of this.

Several minutes passed before the congenial fellow returned, the promised item held out to her. "There you go, miss. Signed by Tyler Preston himself."

"Thanks." She blushed. "I'll bring it up to the register in a minute. I want to look around a little more."

"Take your time," he encouraged and walked over to help another customer.

Curiosity getting the better of her, she slipped open the plastic case and pulled out the inner jacket. Large, splashy printing in heavy black ink covered the bottom corner:

Lori—Have a wonderful Christ-filled Christmas.
And thanks for your support.

How quaint. An illegible scribble followed by what she assumed was his signature. Then another missive caught her eye. It was the same printing but neater, more precise:

Please turn over.

Knitting her brows together in wonder, she flipped open the thin page and discovered yet another handwriting. . .one that looked strangely familiar:

Can't we try just one more time?

Lori felt her heart pick up its pace as she read and reread the brief note. It couldn't be—

"Excuse me," a shaky voice came from behind her. "Would you happen to know where I could find the Purcell CDs?"

She whirled around and met the eyes that had permeated her every thought, her every dream for the last six months. "Spence." The word barely made it through her constricted throat.

He smiled tenderly at her, just the hint of his dimple showing. "How have you been?" He seemed to be the slightest bit hesitant, unsure.

She started to nod her head, but stopped. Then shook it slowly. Now was the time. "Miserable," she admitted.

His eyes softened with concern. "I saw all the. . .I saw the news reports."

"At least it's done," she sighed.

"I was proud of you. You stood up to him. That took courage."

Thinking of the whole airport fiasco, she laughed. "You've no idea."

They stood in uncomfortable silence as they glanced at their surroundings, each seeming to wait for the other to say something.

"Are you—" they both started at the same time and broke off with a nervous laugh.

Spence looked to the floor and back at her, his face more serious. Gingerly, he sought out her hand. "Lori," he said huskily, "I've missed you."

She nodded, pressing her lips together, hoping the tears would stay put.

"I need. . . ," he began. "I need to know if you—"

She sensed what he was going to say. "Spence, I have to tell you something right away. I've met someone."

His expression fell as his eyes probed hers.

"He's really very special. In fact, I'm not quite sure how I lived without Him before."

He dropped her hand and tried to smile through the pained look on his face. "I see. That's. . .great, Lori. I'm sure. . . ." He did not continue.

Lori could endure it no longer. She stepped over to Spence before he turned away and placed a palm against his cheek, gently guiding his face toward her. "I've been talking to Him every day," she said evenly. "Praying that somehow, someway He'd bring you back into my life."

It took several heartbeats for the words to register. When they did, Lori nearly wept with joy at the look of complete surprise on Spence's handsome face.

"You mean. . .you found. . . ?"

"Yes, Spencer. I found the Lord." She paused before continuing. "And I found something else at the same time."

"What?" he whispered.

"This." She smiled through her veil of tears. "I love you, Spencer Berg."

Suddenly, his arms were around her in a fierce hug that left her breathless. Lori realized she had never felt more loved, more safe. . .more at home.

Completely ignoring the curious looks of the rest of the shoppers, Spence dropped to one knee and tenderly kissed her hand. "Lorelei Sommers, will you marry me? Will you be my wife?"

Lori grinned as she nodded her head. "That is one part I have been waiting a long, long time to play."

Several whistles and whoops sounded, and the rest of the onlookers suddenly burst into cheerful applause.

And Lori lost herself in Spence's embrace once more.

A Letter To Our Readers

Dear Reader:

In order that we might better contribute to your reading enjoyment, we would appreciate your taking a few minutes to respond to the following questions. When completed, please return to the following:

Rebecca Germany, Managing Editor
Heartsong Presents
P.O. Box 719
Uhrichsville, Ohio 44683

1. Did you enjoy reading *Behind the Scenes*?
   - ❑ Very much. I would like to see more books by this author!
   - ❑ Moderately
     I would have enjoyed it more if ________________

     ____

2. Are you a member of **Heartsong Presents**? ❑Yes ❑No
   If no, where did you purchase this book? ____________

   ____

3. What influenced your decision to purchase this book? (Check those that apply.)

❑ Cover	❑ Back cover copy
❑ Title	❑ Friends
❑ Publicity	❑ Other________________

4. How would you rate, on a scale from 1 (poor) to 5 (superior), the cover design? ________________

5. On a scale from 1 (poor) to 10 (superior), please rate the following elements.

   __Heroine __Plot

   __Hero __Inspirational theme

   __Setting __Secondary characters

6. What settings would you like to see covered in **Heartsong Presents** books?________________

   ____

   ____

7. What are some inspirational themes you would like to see treated in future books?________________

   ____

   ____

8. Would you be interested in reading other **Heartsong Presents** titles? ❑ Yes ❑ No

9. Please check your age range:
   ❑ Under 18 ❑ 18-24 ❑ 25-34
   ❑ 35-45 ❑ 46-55 ❑ Over 55

10. How many hours per week do you read? ________

Name________________________________

Occupation________________________________

Address________________________________

City________________ State________ Zip________